SACRIFICES INCARNATE

WRITTEN BY:

Christopher M. Fink

This book was edited by Elizabeth Suggs, owner and founder of *Editing Mee*.

Acknowledgments

For Grandma Anne and Grandpa Charlie. Though I know you're not partial to my taste in genre all too much, I wanted to dedicate my first publication to you both. It has always been my wish to create something you could be proud of me for. With that being said, this is for you!

To all my readers, and friends that have helped along the way, your thoughts and notes of my work have helped motivate and sculpt these stories. I hope my love for the genre has connected with you as much as it has with me.

Lastly, but most definitely not least, this book wouldn't have been possible by any stretch without Elizabeth Suggs of *Editing Mee*! To my editor, mentor, and friend, enough cannot be said! Without you, none of this would have happened! I am looking forward to many more projects, and great things in the future! Of my most sincere, and endless gratitude, thank you, Liz!

Brought to you by,

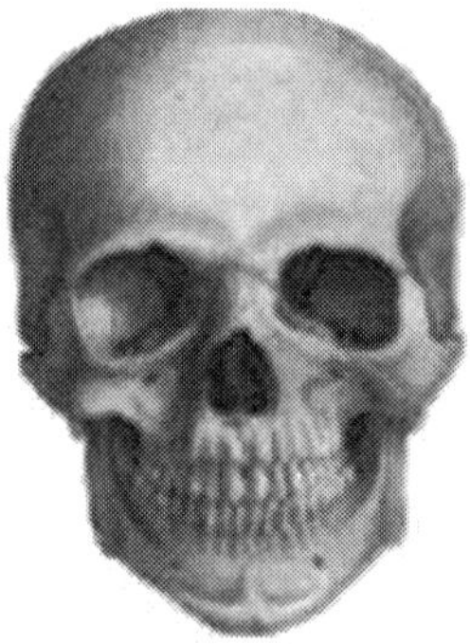

The Horror Seeker

The book which you hold in your hands is more than words put to paper. These people have been created, as well as their respective situations, for reasons I hope that one day can be understood. By opening this book, and engaging their lives, you accept the responsibility of their actions and thus the consequences therein. You do not know these people, and you may never meet them face-to-face; however, this does not absolve your participation in their sorrow. From Laci's encounter with the noxious tar beast of Schoharie County, New York; a journey that had all but stripped away her complacent existence, to Jeremiah's immortal slumber of eternal darkness.

Yes, they've suffered and will continue to do so, as long as these words exist. The disheartening truth is, they must. The question then becomes, can you bear the burden of their torment?

As you will read, there are things among us which you still cannot fully understand; perhaps you're not meant to. However, there are those of us who have found a way to chamber these entities into holding. This book is one such chamber where "they" wait, and the characters within these pages have been created for their... entertainment, if you will. For if they—the entities—had nothing to do, no blood to shed, they would surely find a way to free themselves of this bond. These characters bear the scars, but they do so for your salvation, and the salvation of all humanity. Read at your own peril, and for the sake of all you know and hold dear.

Or, if you're anything like me, sit back and simply enjoy the show!

\- *The Seeker*

Table of Contents:

NO FRACKING

Laci curled up in a tight ball in the small crevasse among the debris of dirt and broken glass. Amid the shower steam, she was tucked between the toilet and shower door; a frigid air creeping through the window.

Sitting in the dark, Laci straightened up, flattening herself against the wall. Still damp, the wall was slick with condensed water, made her efforts to move difficult. A chill crawled through her skin and rattled her bones, made worse at the mere thought of that creature; the black, oily beast; *it reached for me... out of thin air!* Laci remained splayed against the wall, holding herself as far from the window as she could. She hoped whatever this thing was couldn't fit through the small opening, but if she moved, its arm might reach her if it were so determined.

Laci had finally gotten control of her extremities, during which her mind relaxed, and her lungs were able to fill with air. But that smell, the same thing she and Gary had noticed earlier on their way to the Catskills. That vile, putrid odor of burnt oil and metal when Laci had first seen the tar creature—she saw it then, and she knew it now. She knew it was out there. In her mind, in the smallest, most honest recess there was, the area of intuition where you cannot lie to yourself, she knew she was dead, or soon would be. As her tension settled, her emotions rose. She started sobbing heavily, choking on her saliva, trying to inhale. She thought of what it was out there, what it might be; it certainly would explain the sparse population in the area. The abandoned neighborhoods they drove through to get here—ones that looked apocalyptic, eroded and forgotten, as if folks had up and disappeared in an instant some years, perhaps decades ago. She thought of their reasons for coming here in the first place, here to spend a weekend away from their busy lives and demanding schedules, wishing now for nothing more than their normal routine, had they driven through the night to their original destination this wouldn't have been. If she hadn't gone along with her husband's desire to take the scenic route and explore detour after detour, only now did she regret it... she thought of Gary.

Her husband was outside, only a few feet from her, and he couldn't have felt further away. The last image she had of Gary was through the window, just before it had burst open, shards of glass cutting through her face. His misshapen body lay motionless atop a pile of garbage, one of the many heaps scattered about the property.

It was dark, with only the faint moonlight shown overhead; darker still trying to see through a foggy window and tear-filled eyes. But a shimmer of a black liquid, running free from his neck and several long eviscerated gashes through his clothes—they too, now wet and matted against his body, discolored by the same grim, visceral liquid. It was an image she could not purge from her mind. Laci continued to sob uncontrollably in the night silence, fearful of any noise that may alert to her presence.

Slowly—Hyperventilating, Laci pulled herself back up, sliding her back against the wall—her eyes never leaving the window. Standing straight now, she couldn't hear or see anything through the jagged teeth of shattered glass around the black void. Taking cautious and calculated steps, she inched her way to the door holding a breath in her chest.

During the few minutes—minutes that felt like hours, she'd been in the bathroom, her eyes had adjusted to the dark well enough that she could see the vague shapes of all the obstacles in her path. The mold ridden sink, or the rusty toiletry tray above it, or the sharp corners of the towel rail which would have cut across her back if she didn't step off the wall. Laci held her arm outstretched, reaching desperately for the door handle. She turned to make sure she was on track and then glanced one last time at the window, which was almost at her back now. Her hand felt the doorknob, and for the split second she faced the window again, blind to any presence there may still be, a sudden surge of panic threatened to take hold of her body. She fought this as she cracked open the door so she could roll herself out.

Laci slammed the door shut and held tension firm on the handle, as if her effort in doing so made it more secure. She once again slid to the floor, her body held at an angle away from the back wall. Her eyes took a few moments to readjust to the light as she looked around the room. The layers of dust blanketing the outdated furniture; it was confusing before, but made more sense now. Explains why nobody had taken up residence here for some time... or maybe they had.

Another wave of tears ran down her cheeks, ones which she tries to resist, but failed to do so. Her sorrow for her husband was not lost, and even as her thoughts, continued to dampen her motivation to escape Laci was unable to submit willingly to death. *Gary would not want that*, she thought. Laci was not a spiritual person by any sense of the word, but it now became a comforting notion, one she could entertain so far as to make herself believe that her husband was here with her now, watching over her. "I know you're here," she told herself quietly. "I know you're here, babe." Trying to convince herself as she rose and rifled through their duffle bags on the bed. Through tears and sniffles, and short shuddering breaths, Laci searched desperately, panicked, through the clothes and pockets for the keys. "I'm sorry..." she said to no one—to Gary.

She unzipped every side pouch, checked every crevasse of their bags, her pockets, casting aside every article from their bags until they were scattered about the bed, before remembering where they were—Gary had asked for them earlier to get a snack from the car. She knew if she couldn't find them outside near the car, they had to be in his pocket. Laci looked to the wall, *through* the wall—visualizing where Gary's body lay on the other side, silently cursing the universe for her predicament. *WHY?! WHY IS THIS HAPPENING TO ME?!*

Back to square one, Laci reached over the bed hastily grabbing her phone off the end table, nearly snapping the cord in two. She curled up between the two beds and the desk behind her, insulated on three sides; she felt as though she were backed against the wall of a narrow alleyway. Thinking on who to call, she was dumbfounded, wondering why she hadn't made the obvious call... she dialed, and the line rang once before an operator picked up:

"911, what is your emergency?" a young male voice said plainly.

"Yes, my name is Laci Nichols," she began quietly under hissing short breaths, but relieved to hear another voice, "I'm trapped in my motel room in... I... there's something outside! I can't leave. Please! You got to get someone out here, please!"

"Okay, Ma'am. I need you to calm down for me." Laci tried to slow her breathing. "Is there anyone else there with you?"

"My husband, Gary Nichols. He... he went out to our car, and he's... he's..." Laci couldn't finish the sentence.

"Okay, Ma'am. Can you tell me where you are?" The dispatcher said calmly.

"I don't know. We're in a motel in the Catskills. I don't know the address."

"Okay, I want you to stay on the line with me. Everything will be fine." The dispatcher said reassuringly, "Now, is there anyone around that you can see? Anyone that can stay with you?"

Laci slowly stood up and made her way to the front window. Nervously, she pulled the blinds apart just enough to peek outside; part of her felt that it would be on the other side of the glass, staring back at her with those toxic yellowed eyes. Thankfully not, but there was a dim light coming from the window across the parking lot under the neon lit sign OFFICE, which burned red over the awning.

"I think there's still someone in the office."

"Okay, if you're able, if it's safe, I need you to go there and stay put."

Go outside?!

"I'll find out where you are and have a car dispatched soon."

"Okay," Laci said, and the line went quiet.

Holding a silent phone to her ear, Laci looked out the window again, waiting for the nerve that would allow her to attempt the journey. She looked left, then right, and back and forth again, hoping to see any sign of life around—there was none. In her gut, she knew the reason for there being nothing outside. The creature's presence kept everything away.

The door crept open an inch at a time until Laci was able to lean out, her right hand braced on the back of the door ready to slam it shut if need be. It was an eerie silence, not a sound from any nightly creature; no crickets, no birds, only the soft rustling of the leaves blowing in the wind. The autumn air of upstate New York was frigid, cutting through her clothes, while her damp hair ran icy water down her back.

Holding the phone on her neck now, Laci looked around; it was clear. Laci cautiously stepped out of her room, away from the little sanctity it provided. She took a few steps into the parking lot, past a decomposing pick-up truck; it was rusted beyond salvage and sitting askew with its bumper propped on the curb, and on all four flat tires, the rubber shredded and decayed from the rims. This was such the condition of the other seven vehicles (except for theirs), a sight she so easily neglected to acknowledge when they arrived. She saw it before, but it was much more prominent now. It's so strange how memory works. This truck, though, was more than a grim image, it greatly resembled a pick-up in a similar condition left in the weeds off of route twenty-eight coming into the area. Its body was weathered and rusted, sunken to the ground, almost completely hidden by the surrounding vegetation. Alongside the driver's side panel a graphic was crudely spray-painted in bright orange: NO FRACKING. It was an ominous protest they had crossed several times on the road. Many signs were staked along driveways with the word FRACK behind a circle and slash, and several other areas with the stern warning; there was nothing subtle about it. And here, Laci noticed, the same damning proclamation in oversized, bold letters and faded red paint scrolled across the wall of the first six units of the building NO FRACKING.

Pretty serious, she thought. She wondered if it might be in part related to what was happening here. The thing that was stalking her—*were there more*? Laci didn't have time to think about it, now coming to the office door. She tried the doorknob, it was locked. Trying several more times, frantically hoping it would give. When that didn't work, she pounded on the door until her fist ached. Overhead, the neon office sign drew out a sustained tone *zzzzzzzzzzzz*... shrouding her in a dim red light. Laci put the phone to her ear, "Hello?" The line was still quiet. She lowered the phone and moved to the office window, slamming her fist on the Plexiglas.

"Hello, Mrs. Nichols?" The young dispatcher came back on the line.

"Yes," Laci almost screamed, "I'm here! Please, tell me you're on the way." She went back to knocking on the window.

"Ma'am, are you with anyone?"

"I'm trying. There's no one here," she said on the verge of tears. She moved again to knock on the door, trying the handle again, and then back to the window.

"Did you say that your husband was there with you? Where is he?"

"He's dead! Alright?" she said, knocking desperately on the window. "Please, you have to send someone."

Laci smacked harder on the pane hoping she could break through. Finally, a light came on from the back room. It shone through the small port-hole window of the door behind the counter. Laci came to attention, waiting to see someone. A portly Hispanic woman came into view, the same woman that checked them in. She was only tall enough to just see into the window. Laci beckoned her to come out and let her in. She could see, though, the woman was angrily waving her away, before leaving herself and shutting off the light.

"No!" Laci screamed. "Open the door!"

"Ma'am? Mrs. Nichols," the dispatch operator called to her, "Can you tell me where you are?" Laci listened, turning back to face the parking lot.

"What? No." Laci was a stir, "It's called the Catskill motel. I don't remember the address."

"I think I know of it," the dispatch operator said, "but it's going to take us some time to get out to you."

"No, please." Laci became erratic, coughing and choking. She had to shield her nose from the rancid tar smell that had seeped around her. She remembered it... "There's something here! It killed my husband, and it's gonna kill me! You have to send somebody."

"I will report your location and situation, and we'll get someone to you as soon as possible," the dispatcher reassured, "but for now I need you to remain inside. Go back to your room and lock the doors. Someone will be there soon."

Frightened, Laci spoke under her breath, "I can't stay here!"

"You'll be fine, ma'am. Please listen..." there was a pause, "go back to your room and lock the door. Someone will be there soon, okay?"

Laci closed her phone scanning the area. She was abandoned. No husband, no hotel staff, no police. Despite the assurance that help was coming, she felt no more secure now than a few moments ago.

Laci coughed louder. The smell was more engrossing by the second, almost to the point where she couldn't breathe at all. She pinched her nose and closed her mouth, staring back at her room. *I can't go back there*. Still, it was her only option. She made a move toward her room, when a gravely, throaty growl, rolled over her shoulder. Its breath coating her body, as Laci instinctively turned to look at it. Her eyes blurred until only the shape of the creature came to form. Lanky, with a wide torso, its imposing stature stood hunched under the shallow overhang of the building. It was all she cared to see before making a dash across the parking lot to her car.

Please, be there. Please! Laci prayed in her mind, prayed that the keys would be on the ground somewhere, somewhere where Gary had dropped them. She reached the car and found that the back door was still open, and their food bag had spilled out onto the ground. She dropped to one knee and sifted through the debris, hopeful, but found nothing. Leaning further, looking under the chassis there was nothing more. Her heart sank, knowing the last place the keys could be. At the same time, when the question of whether or not she'd be able to face the gruesome sight of her husband's deformed body was circling in her mind, her eyes caught a dark liquid running slowly down the curb in front of the car. Though hesitant admit, she knew it was blood, and worse, where it came from. The true terror of what had happened moments ago was taking shape.

Laci cinched her coat tighter as she came around to the open front door. She dreaded the sight around every turn but forced herself to look, still convinced she might find the keys. What remained of the decrepit phone booth was in pieces. It was one of those old-timey glass ones, tall with the word PHONE in a blue box above. Glass was shattered and strewn about all over the ground, and the metal was severely bent out of shape by some tremendous force. It leaned at an extreme angle against the building, and the devastating sight of the blood that ran down the left side of the only intact pane of glass brought Laci to shuddering tears once again. She could imagine Gary's body leaning out of the broken frame before being taken in back, dragged as it appeared to be, as she followed a marbled trail of blood around the building. She only hoped there was no pain; the only thing beyond wishing this all never happened at all.

She had to leave; she knew that and willed herself along following the trail around back. She didn't look down; she didn't have to. Fighting through the fear, she pressed onward toward a storage shed. Laci stepped over several pieces of rubbish left to rot until coming around to the over grown patch of grass in back.

It was a narrow passage behind the motel next to a small rise that rolled above and over into the woods. It was dark and suffocating, and Laci paused a moment to reestablish herself, having lost the blood trail in the tall weeds. She could see ahead of the broken wood and garbage slope outside her window, where she knew Gary lay dead. Even more disturbing, a motion sensor light from the corner of the office building, out of view from her vantage point, shined its cold blue glow over the sight as if to guide her way. Taking her first steps forward, she tried not to think of what she might see; remembering now that the light hadn't been on before.

Laci was on high alert for any sign of that creature; the smell, the sound of its raspy breath, the fear it brought with it. She wondered how something so impenetrable to the sense could hide so well. It had to be here, watching… waiting. Was she blind to it or was it blind to her?

As Laci neared Gary's body, she fought against the tremors in her own. Nervous, and with a chill that seemed to follow her. *Is that it? Is it following me?* Was it fear that made it visible? She didn't know, and the thought of such a method of hunting made her very uneasy.

Something rustled in the bushes beyond the hill. She whipped around to the noise. It was there! Laci turned back around and realized she was now standing over Gary, his condition in full detail. Laci saw the lacerations from the glass, but the others were unknown. Three large punctures, roughly an inch in diameter had pierced through him. She could envision the talon that reached for her earlier. It would match these wounds, as if this is how the creature had carried Gary back here. She pictured his dead weight being toted behind the building.

She knelt down beside Gary and put her hand on his shoulder in a comforting manner, as if to say (under ordinary circumstances) *everything's going to be okay. I'm here for you.* His body was still warm, for the moment. She drew her hand back, noticing the blood running down her palm. Laci hyperventilated, almost forgetting why she was here, *the keys!* Against her panic, she patted down his pockets feeling through the dampened patches of blood. She came up to his jacket pocket hung by a literal thread. She took hold and felt something sharp; it jingled as she tried to pull the fabric away completely. It didn't give, Laci reached in, touching the cold metal of the car keys. She was home free, but the idea of leaving him behind now stalled her momentum. She looked down at her husband once again, feeling guilty, even responsible to a degree for what had happened. It could have been her; *it should've been me*, the thought passed through her mind. She almost didn't notice the pocket of warm air that had begun to shroud her. It was only when the coughing returned that Laci noticed the beast, by then it was too late. Soft cavernous breaths dusted across her shoulder, taking hers away in the process. Its breath drew itself over her neck; she froze, and turned slowly to face it, her bones felt rusted solid.

Even under the creature's body, Laci felt the cold move right through her. Her body shook, and she could feel the frigid moisture gathering on her skin and tears running free from her eyes, but she was not crying, now inches from the thing staring back at her. Its oily mass and thin boney limbs attached to its broad lurching torso. It looked her up and down; it seemed to be examining her, curious. Its shoulders heaved with every breath, and yes, that smell, the same as before only now it was near crippling. Laci choked on what little air she was able to pull into her lungs. She remained propped on her knees, staring right through the beast, trying to pretend it wasn't there, hoping the creature might lose interest if she didn't move. What little control she had left of her body, she was able to shoot a glance upward but couldn't see its eyes. In this light, its eyes blended well with its reptilian black skin, crusted over its body. The creature was still, before taking in a sharp raspy inhale of air, its body snapping erect as if something odd had caught its nose. Laci reacted and shot backward, tripping on loose garbage, and falling violently to the ground. She hit her head against a piece of two by four that protruded from the garbage heap. Almost instantly, she was knocked out cold. The image of the creature was the last thing she saw before everything faded to black.

***

Laci came to in the early morning light, her head and shoulders wracked with pain. She took her time, rolling herself up onto one hand, then to a knee. For a moment, she had to remember where she was, glancing around the cloud of the thick fog that hung in the air. She looked next to her, where Gary's mutilated body once laid, now only a stain of blood that dripped through the cracks of the garbage pile. It trailed off over the hill and into the woods. At her feet, she picked up the keys, and wanting to see nothing more of this, she willed herself up, her head pounding, and slowly made her way back around the front. Brushing through the tall grass, the heavy dew gathered on her shoes and leaked in, chilling her body more than it already was. She shivered.

Laci limped around the corner and saw the property now in a hazy light; it somehow seemed more ghoulish in the motionless fog. From the far end of the lot, she could barely make out the office building. She took slow deliberate steps toward her car, passing by the macabre sight of the booth and the blood.

She leaned against the car's bumper, assisting herself to the ground and sat against the car door. Exhausted, emotionally, and physically, Laci sat sprawled out on the asphalt, waiting for what may come. Be it death or rescue, she had no more energy for either. The area was as silent as it had been during the night, but there was something different. Far out in the distance, something was cutting through the trees. A siren! Either by luck or design, she had survived the night; now she hoped she could only survive the memory.

"Untitled"

Although the sound was dampened on the fourth floor, each bullet fired carried a pulse of panic. Even from the east wing, the percussion boomed through the building, as did the intermittent tremors that came from below. Picture frames knocked from the walls and all manner of trinkets fell from counters and tables, as if the building were shaken by a great force, crumbling from within. Startled awake and alert in their beds, patients sat in terrified uncertainty; many of them in such fragile condition that the simple task of sitting upright took effort. Nurses tirelessly hurried from room to room, doing what they could to keep people calm and moving the more critical patients away from the pandemonium.

In the hall, doctors and staff quickly maneuvered through the distressed patients who were guided toward the nearest exit. Some stood by, nervous, waiting with orderlies while several more lay helpless their in beds, which lined the walls all along the corridor. Security guards assisted where they could by moving those who were able to the exits, trying to keep the scene as organized as possible, waving people to the stairwell with repeated assurances of comfort.

"Doctor..." a nurse called out from a room.

The doctor entered and stood in the doorway facing a petite looking woman, strands of her hair had torn from her braid, and her uniform disheveled. A glaze of sweat developing on her forehead reflected her urgent efforts. She stood at the far end of the room behind a bed she had just pulled in, this being the third bed in a room built to accommodate only two. The patient was a middle-aged woman, sedated due to her injury. The other two were a fragile old man in his late eighties, and an elderly African woman, also in her eighties. Both were awake and anxious from the commotion, compounded further when hearing the nurse speaking to the doctor.

"What's happening?" the nurse asked. "I'm running out of space! We can't fit more than three gurneys to a room."

"Make it work, Janet!" the doctor ordered, slicing his hand through the air; there would be no further objection. "However many you can fit; whatever you have to do. I need everyone out of the hall—now!"

"Excuse me?" the older man asked, raising his hand. "May I have some water, please?"

"Janet, here, will attend to you, sir," the doctor answered hurriedly.

Janet continued to position the beds in the most accommodating way she could, adjusting equipment and making the best use of the space. She approached the older gentleman's bed to pour a cup of water, handing it to him with a smile as another tremor shook the foundation.

"What is that?" the man asked, with a slight worry to his voice.

"It's nothing, sir. Just try to relax. We have everything under control." Janet did her best to sound convincing, but even she didn't believe her own words.

"Nurse?" the woman's gravelly voice asked from behind the dividing curtain. Janet made her way around to the woman who was sitting up in bed. Her thin white hair pulled back in a tight bun that looked to have been that way for years. The woman in her frail condition did her best to positon herself comfortably before presenting the phone to Janet. "Nurse, my phone isn't working," the woman reported.

"I'm sorry, ma'am," Janet regretfully stated. "We have an alert situation which is affecting our power and phone lines. They'll be fixed as soon as possible, okay?"

Unsatisfied, the woman let out a disappointed sigh and returned to her own world. Janet hurried around the room, continuing to check monitors and consolidate equipment. She drew the curtains about half way across the foot of the beds and the same for the center divider, giving all three patients some measure of privacy.

Now confined to her own corner the old woman settled into her bed and peered out the window, which overlooked the entrance to the hospital.

Police cruisers and SWAT lined the length of the road. However, at this angle her field of vision was limited. From what she could see, the police cruisers bathed the surrounding area in a dazzling array of blue and red light, flaring out most of the people being lead out of the hospital;

some she could see, frenzied and panicked, running in all directions.

As the last of the patients exited into the stairwell, a security guard took a quick walk up and down the hall, checking for stragglers, and then flagged the doctor down.

"Is there anyone left?" the security guard snapped.

"No, no," the doctor answered. "Those who are remaining are being secured in their rooms. I'm going to stay and keep it together up here. I have a few nurses to help if I need anything."

The doctor continued forward, as the guard moved the last of the patrons into the stairwell before closing and locking the access door. Turning back, the guard inspected each room as he passed, maneuvering through the quickened pace of the attendees.

A sudden crash rumbled the structure of the hospital, and resonated throughout the floor, knocking everyone to their knees and into the walls. All manner of loose papers and supplies shook from their stations as several gunshots rang out. Patients and staff fell to their knees in terror, looking every which way anticipating the next happening; many clung to whatever was within arm's reach for stability. The guard came to his feet first, helping others up along the way as he continued down the hall. Finally, a call came over his radio:

"Is there anyone left on three or four?" the man's scream came through the radio.

The guard picked up his microphone, "This is Murray. I'm on four. Who is this?"

"This is Kendrick!" the man responded. "I'm in the north stairwell on two, down the hall from the maternity ward."

"I'm heading toward the north wing right now," Murray said. "What's going on? Do you know what that quake was?"

"I need backup down here!" Kendrick barked. "Keep everyone away from the north wing. Send everyone out toward the main entrance."

"What's happening?" Murray demanded. "People are starting to panic up here!"

Murray maneuvered through personnel and debris, running by Janet along the way. She took a few steps then stopped and turned toward Murray.

"Sir!" Janet called out, trying to control her frustration, "Can you please tell me what's happening?"

Murray stopped to address Janet. "Ma'am, I'm not sure. Just keep everyone secure and headed east. No one heads to the north wing, okay?" Murray began to stride away, leaving Janet to her duties.

Rounding the corner, he passed by the receptionist's area where nurses hastily rifled through papers. Approaching the north stairwell, several people pushed past Murray and down the stairwell.

"Hey!" Murray called out. "I need you to exit down the east stairwell. Take the main entrance out."

The people ran on by heading east as Murray opened the stairwell door and peered down the tan column. The faded green rubber track that ran the middle of each step was free of dust, and no debris had fallen or crumbled from the walls. The area was well insulated, and apart from the commotion in the hall behind him, it was deserted. Sporadic blasts of gunfire echoed from below and carried up the column. Again, a low rumble vibrated up the corridor, followed by several more distant gunshots that Murray could feel in his chest. He drew his gun and held it at attention, pointing down the stairs prepared for anything that might pose as a threat. With his free hand, he took hold of his microphone.

"Kendrick?" Murray called hopefully.

He waited for a response apprehensively listening for any more gunfire or anything out of the ordinary. More shots rang out from an unknown distance. However, they seemed to be moving away, as well as the continued rumbling that followed each occurrence. Once the disturbance ceased, Kendrick responded.

"I don't know—I don't know what it is!" Kendrick hissed. "It just came through the wall!"

Confused, it took Murray a moment to respond, "Did you say it came *through* the wall?" He stepped into the stairwell, standing at the edge of the first step. Listening and waiting. "Kendrick?" Murray again called into his radio.

"Hold on," Kendrick responded, sounding less panicked. "I'm gonna check on something."

"Just hang on," Murray said as he descended the stairs "I'm on my way to you."

Thoughts entered Murray's head as he made his way down, specifically the "*it*" in Kendrick's statement. "*It*" came through the wall. Something was alive—something unknown. As Murray descended the stairs, images of bad 40's horror movies filled his mind in an effort to encapsulate what was down there. A giant leech... a radioactive reptile... or even an oversized human causing the destruction just below his position. These were images he used to laugh at; yet, under the circumstances, it became a legitimate thought. How would he fend off such a creature? Once he recognized that these were ridiculous scenarios, the thought of a hand or tentacle coming from the floor and pulling him down; he proceeded forward. Every so often, another rumble would come up through the walls, and Murray would crouch down with a white knuckle grip on the rail to secure himself. *What is that,* he thought. More shots rang out from below, and Murray got an equally tighter grip on his pistol. Coming around the first corner, Murray stood atop the next set of stairs. Painted in dark green on the adjacent wall was an oversized three above the access door below. Still, aside from the audible disturbances, nothing seemed out of place here. For the moment, though, the noise seemed to retreat to a lull. No time to relax, though, now at the base of the stairs, he opened the door to check for any disturbances.

A quick look around revealed the same scene as the fourth floor; the confusion was equally present. However, the physical disturbance appeared more prevalent.

Murray glanced over at an approaching nurse. "Nurse..." Murray flagged her down. "Is everything alright here?"

"I don't know," she said, trying to catch her breath, "We're doing what we can. But we don't have the resources."

"Anyone that is able..." Murray said "Should head to the east wing. Tell everyone to avoid this stairwell and the E.R., understand?"

The nurse nodded and carried on as Murray stepped back in the stairwell and closed the door. He turned and continued down. Rounding the corner and descending the stairs to the second floor, Murray slowed his pace, taking more caution as he came to the area where Kendrick had been reporting. He stopped at the base of the first set of stairs. A thick sort of bile smell putrefied the air around him with a sick sort of texture. Murray did his best to keep his composure as he came around to face the second-floor descent. From here, he could see the first signs of the devastation. He paused for a moment to try Kendrick again.

"Kendrick?" he called into his radio, uncertain of the situation.

Murray waited for several moments, but Kendrick never answered. By the condition of the floor below and Kendrick's lack of response, Murray made his own bleak assumptions. He took a breath before stepping down. Fractures ran up the stairwell walls, stretching from the access door, which was broken out from its fixture, leaving a hole almost twice its size. *What could have done this?* Murray thought as he brought his gun up in front of him. The lights sporadically flashed from the hall, giving him an idea of what to expect. The emergency lighting console was torn from its fixture, spitting sparks from the exposed wiring. The wall in front of him gone, leaving a large misshapen depression in the rock beneath the dark green 2 painted above. He observed blotches of a thick red fluid dripping from the jagged parts of the concrete as if something had cut itself. The same liquid ran under the rubble a bit more freely like a river, running past and following down the stairwell. *A water main must've broken.* Carefully, he stepped onto the debris and looked around the corner down the next staircase. To his disbelief, the inside rail and half the stairwell had crumbled to the next level below. There is no way down from here.

Murray stepped carefully over the debris and into the hall of the second floor. At first glance, the carnage was incalculable. The sight was the likeness of two worlds standing side by side. While only a few feet from the corridor, it seemed to be in order. Murray could see staff and patients alike scurrying here and there down the hall. The immediate area, however, was a section shrouded in darkness and destruction. The receptionist's area in front of him lay in ruins; the support columns broken in half, and the desk with all its contents destroyed. Papers stained with blood were torn and blown about the area along with several pieces of electrical equipment that lay to waste, ripped from their fixtures, and tossed aside into the adjacent hall. There was no one around; however, Murray got a glimpse of a nurse beneath the wreckage; she was lying face down—unresponsive. Her body twisted in such a way it was fair to assume she couldn't be alive. A stream of blood ran free from under the body, coming from the lacerations on her back, and the missing arm, perhaps severed by the mound of rubble atop of her. Her body plunged through the structure by something that had taken a vicious grip around her torso, nearly splitting her in two.

The infrequent flashes of electrical shorting light only revealed brief glimpses of the carnage. Murray shielded himself from the brutality and moved on to his right, further into the dark. More non-descript fractures and depressions lined the walls and ceiling, the floor was a familiar traitorous foundation of debris similar to what was in the stairwell. Metal siding and support rails were snapped and twisted into knots with gurneys and wheelchairs flattened. The next several yards lie in darkness, interrupted by flashing and the sparks of several light fixtures from the exposed ceiling. A nearby pipe had burst from a concaved water fountain responsible for the flooding that lead through the stairs. Murray observed the damage all around in shock; the same thick red substance hung from every jagged corner and smeared along the wall—or what remained of *it*—as the river, now mostly blood, ran beneath the rubble.

Ahead, Murray could see the area from which the mayhem must've begun; an entire section of the wall blown out, giving way to the devastation of the operating room. It appeared the same as the surrounding area, only here it was a significantly more macabre sight. Among the lamps, monitors, tools and equipment thrashed about, lay the two doctor's ravaged bodies recognizable only by their scrubs. They were buried under the scattered remains of a room once used to save lives; it now stood as a depiction of death. The sight was a grim display of eviscerated bodies. Some savagely pulverized into the foundation, with blood splatter and limbs scattered about; a center stage for some twisted play that only the most heinous of sociopathic minds could appreciate. Fixed under the primary surgical lamp, a woman lay on a gurney, her legs hanging off either side. Her torso ripped in half from pelvis to chest.

It was impossible to comprehend what could have caused such trauma. Then, Murray had recalled the brief exchange he had made with Kendrick before he went quiet: "It just came through the wall." *It*? Murray invited every imaginative creature into the room that "*it*" could possibly be. Further inspection revealed "*it*" had to come from the woman herself, from inside her? *She birthed it?* Murray shivered. He didn't have time to assess what had happened. Below, Murray could hear the destructive racket and continued on.

A swift turn around, perhaps with a bit of extra motivation to escape the room, he hurried back to the stairwell to see if there was any way to reach the next level down from here. A glance suggested the damage was too severe, so he opted to turn back and head to the east stairwell. He quickened his pace as he approached the surgical room, not wanting to catch a peripheral glimpse of the carnage.

At the other end of the hall, Murray reached the access door. Here, the scene was quiet, having been evacuated, with only a few loose items knocked from their perch. *It's amazing*, he thought, *the difference in atmosphere*, knowing of the hell that was only a few yards behind him. From this vantage point, it appeared as though the section of the hall suffered a simple power outage, but Murray knew differently. For someone who hadn't seen it for themselves there was no way of conveying the horror, nor would he ever want to.

The east stairwell was vacant, only the distant cries and exclamations echoing up; everyone who could make it out had done so. Murray moved with an even greater urgency down the stairs, with his pistol in hand, he held the weapon at his shoulder. Gunfire continued to echo softly, and he paused for a moment, taking caution before rounding the corner. Now facing the descent to the first-floor, he could see nothing but the illumination from the hall from the open door. There were no guards, no police, no staff, and no patients remaining at the scene. Down the stairs, he flattened himself against the wall under the oversized 1 painted on the wall above. From here, the hallway that ran around the corner and out of view was undisturbed and empty. The pair off doors visible, were closed, and undoubtedly locked.

Murray took a breath and gathered his courage, preparing himself for what he was about to face. He bent his body slightly around the doorframe, seeing the mussel flashes of automatic weapons and several officers attempting to bear down on whatever... creature, he assumed, was out of view.

The officer's uniforms looked tactical, fully loaded with riot gear; *had to be SWAT*, he thought, or some other specialized response team. He debated for several moments whether or not he should interfere, but curiosity, the ever-prodding devil, got the better of him. Such a situation took place in this hospital, coupled with the devastation and traumatic scenes in the rooms above; he had to know what was responsible.

He willed himself around the corner and made his way down the corridor, his pistol ready, staying close to the far wall. With his knowledge of the hospital, he knew that if there was something up ahead trying to escape, it would have to turn left toward the emergency room lobby. If he could get close enough, he may be able to see it. Several special unit officers were positioned just ahead of him firing short bursts of rounds into the dark, each followed by a low, bellowing groan. It was the sound of suffering and pain. Whatever this thing was, it was hurting, and angry! Murray stopped in his tracks a few feet from the darkened hall. The only lights available were the ones mounted atop of the officer's rifles, all trained on the monstrous pulsing creature stuck in the hall. The detail was limited, a bulging mass of flesh; it looked like an oversized heart heaving rhythmically, as if it were breathing. It was difficult to make out, but Murray thought he could see something crawling out along the walls and the ceiling.

The nearest officer suddenly fell onto his back, landing with a jerk as if something had pulled his legs out. He disappeared into the shadows screaming, and then silence. The remaining two team members resumed firing, aiming in all directions with more desperation. Murray watched as the mussel flashes winked out, and the lights of the guns fell to the floor. Again, there were quick belches of screams... until there weren't anymore. The creature heaved as it struggled to move. Murray began firing at the monster, with only the accidental, yet convenient placement of the rifle light to guide him, its beam trained on the creature. Murray unloaded his clip with little to no effect. As he went to reload his weapon, unaware of the tentacle arm slithering above, he fired several more rounds before it caught his eye. He managed to squeeze off two aimless shots until the arm came down and slammed him against the wall with such an impact leaving an imprint in the reinforced sheetrock. He fell to the floor and blacked out.

***

Several minutes later, Murray recovered, gripping his side tight as he brought himself to his feet. Each breath came with a shock of pain, not since he was in his early twenties had he broken his ribs, but he never forgot how it felt.

He carried himself toward the exit, fighting the pain as he followed the screams. Without his gun, there wasn't much he could do to stop it, though he still had to know what it was. The pain he felt was excruciating. It didn't matter now; there was no doctor or nurse around to be his proxy of better judgment. He followed the path of destruction, with rock and drywall still falling from the ceiling, accompanied by live wires dangling from the above fixtures. An explosion of glass from down the hall quickened Murray's pace. The pain, however, still had him moving rather slow.

The screams and a heavy hail of gunfire rang out, halting Murray in his tracks. He used the time to catch his breath, wincing as the pain continued to persist. Several bullets made their way through, sending shards of debris all around, as Murray took a few decided steps to the side away from the line of fire. After a moment, it ceased, so he moved forward cautiously.

Making his way through the lobby; what he saw was nothing—nothing but devastation. A hollow path was burrowed through the emergency room, and through the entrance, the hanging metal frames and a carpet of shattered glass and blood were all that remained.

Murray took slow limping steps toward the distant screams, and the concussive sounds from the street. Car alarms flared up and fires raged in its wake.

He emerged from the doorway and looked around at the defeated police force, scrambling together what was left of their unit to continue their pursuit to try and stop it. Murray stood there, taking in what air his chest would allow without agony. No one had ever seen this coming, or even knew what to make of it. What was the creature? Did it have a purpose? One thing was certain—it was alive! Surely it needed to sleep, drink... eat. Sooner or later, it will need to settle down, somewhere.

RESTLESS

It couldn't have been long...

Or, at least that was Jerimiah's best guess. The fact that he was still alive was a clear indication of that. Blackness; nothing but dense darkness surrounded him. He tried to maneuver, but space was limited; in fact, he was barely able to separate his arms from his body. Lifting his hand, he jammed his thumb on the roof, only inches above him. Several times he would bang on the roof as hard as he could; the stiff sound of his strikes unable to resonate through the uncertain surface that lay on top of him. He inspected himself up and down; a suit, a tie, and even his Yamaka. It all started to sink in, albeit as hard a notion it was to comprehend.

Hyperventilating—the sound of his breathing brushing along the walls of his congested quarter, he tried desperately to remember what he could. Where was he before this? How did this happen? Why couldn't he remember anything? He began to thrash and kick about, hoping for something to give way. All these questions and more raced through his mind, but none as terrifying as the most apparent fact: he was buried alive! Jerimiah let out several bellows, screaming in short bursts as the air began to deplete in quality; the smell and taste of his expended breaths taking its place. He knew he had only a few minutes, or less, accounting for the amount of time he'd been here already.

He attempted to claw his way through the roof. This did nothing but bruise his fingers as they now began to bleed; the dampness of his blood mashed within the padded lining of the roof. Jerimiah ripped and clawed at the padding, trying to give himself a sense of progress in his escape. He managed to separate a piece of fabric with his thumb and fore-finger, tearing it from the seam from the corner. Jerimiah did his best to feel out the edges, taking a firm grip of the exposed lining, he pulled with what strength and leverage he could muster. He managed to pull away a large section of fabric of about two square feet. Though he couldn't see anything, the feeling of making headway was encouraging. He patted the slab of wood above him, trying to hear any semblance of an echo, a vibration of any kind that would give him a sense of hope. His blows, however hard, fell flat, yet despite this, Jerimiah pounded until his muscles were numb, crying and laughing in a growing uncontrollable hysteria.

All he could think of was how he could've ended up here. Amongst the tears and the sharp breaths, he tried to imagine how and why someone could've made such a mistake. Did they think he was dead? Why? What had happened? What was the last thing he could remember? Nothing. There was nothing he could recall. He never really did anything out of the ordinary; his routine was pretty standard. He only had two friends he could speak of, or at least those he would go out of his way to spend time with. His best friend Dan, who he spoke to on and off during the week and would drop by his house every so often...

When did I talk to him last? It was... God, when was it? Thursday... Friday? He thought back as best he could remember; he hadn't heard from Dan in days, probably due to the obvious circumstance.

What about Trish? Surely she must realize he's not around. Jerimiah kept in better contact with her. They had a much longer history and were a pair that could share more intimate details. Whatever the reason for this, he was sure Trish had to know of it in some manner. There were nights upon nights when Jerimiah couldn't sleep that he would be able to call her and talk for however long until... *I never could sleep*, he began to recall.

Jerimiah suffered from chronic insomnia, only able to sleep a few hours a night, if at all. There were times where he even went on two, three days without a wink. By that third day, his delirium and disorientation were in full swing. However, that following night's sleep was never better for him, but the years of such a condition had really taken its toll. *There was something...* he thought, *the drug trials!* It was starting to come back.

He had visited the hospital recently for yet another complaint about a string of sleepless nights. With his prescription filled, Jerimiah left for home. Once there, he sat at his computer to turn off his brain for a while. A few hours of web browsing often helped aid in his sleeplessness. However, this night had been different. He received an e-mail about a new drug that was being put into human trials. It was said to be a long term treatment for insomnia; at this point, he was willing to try anything. Typical sleeping pills managed to take the edge off for a while, but Jerimiah was in the market for something sustainable, something he could rely on. The list of side-effects was typical; headaches, muscle weakness and stiffness, joint pain, and such, it was a fair gamble. Nowhere on that list, however, did it mention being buried alive. Still, he could only wonder how it came to this.

The trial...

I had taken the meds, and...

The congestion continued to weigh on Jerimiah, almost as if he could feel the pressure of the earth suffocating him. He tried desperately to shorten his breathing to prolong his life as much as he could. Continuously, he would tap the far end of the coffin with his toe to give himself a readable dimension of his spacing; there wasn't much to go on, nothing had changed, but the continuous inspection gave him something to focus on.

When he had regained some strength in his arms, he felt around the torn area and ripped away more of the fabric. His efforts quickly became frantic, trying desperately to taste fresh air. He found himself holding his breath, unwilling to poison himself further, until he could hold it no longer.

As the dementia began to settle in, his thoughts became more panic-stricken and unnerved. He continued to laugh hysterically, gripping his hair and squeezing it tightly, pulling his scalp up as the hair ripped from his head. He flailed and convulsed, striking all areas of the coffin with disturbed and erratic movements.

He began to realize and understand his fate now. In a few moments, he would pass out and die soon after. In an ironic sense, his insomnia was cured; however, he would have preferred a different method. *Still, how did this happen?* Answers would provide some comfort, at least.

He could only recall one treatment he participated in. It had to be recent, as recent as only a few days ago.

I remember, he thought, *being in the room*. Several other patients, sitting around him in a lab with two doctors who presented their latest treatment for sleep deprivation: "Saltovil." The tests were reported to show promise and were ready to be taken to human trials. The risks were clear, and the money was intriguing. The profits for being a guinea pig weren't a get-rich-quick scheme by any means, but it was a way to pull in some fast cash when needed, as Jerimiah did. With his job slashing hours, he had lost a significant amount of income, and the stress only added to his insomnia; not able to think clearly, his struggles turned to desperation. A simple dose of two pills one hour before intending to sleep was all the instruction they were given. They would return after thirty days of treatment to report their results. As it turns out, he was not able to make that meeting.

Thirty days! Had it been that long?

It couldn't have been; he'd most certainly be dead by now. What then? What was the last thing he could remember? From his first meeting in the lab, he went home and went about his routine until it was time to sleep. He settled down and... *Ugh*, the images became so fuzzy. Nothing was clear. Did he even take the medication? Did he take the wrong ones? Did they give him the wrong ones?! Curiosity turned to anger when the possibility occurred to him that someone else's mistake could've put him here.

He broke into hysterical tears before the laughs started again. The sheer reality of what had happened was absolutely absurd. Wasn't he examined thoroughly enough before his burial? Well, as far as Jewish tradition goes, the dead are to be buried within a day or two of death. But where had he been beforehand?

Jerimiah coughed. The air was becoming increasingly toxic. He knew he would be dead soon. *Damn it!* Hadn't the company done a thorough enough check with its subjects? There must've been more that had suffered the same disturbing fate as him. Were they buried, too? They had to be! *A cover-up!* His brain ran from rational to senselessness. One moment he would be in tears, then a sudden lash out at the coffin - in a sense at the world - then to fits of laughter. As the air grew thicker, he began to babble to himself,

"Someone had to have seen me before this. No one noticed me breathing? How?!"

His anger grew, "Accept the fact that Jeremy's dead. No one cares! Just bury the fucker! Right!?!" He coughed some more. *This was it*, he thought. The air tasted bad, very polluted. Jerimiah felt the urge to throw up. He held it back as long as he could, but the sensation was too much as he turned his head as far to the right as his neck would allow and retched, immediately the smell only made matters worse. He coughed again, spitting up whatever was left inside him. The vomit sat in a puddle next to his ear, and he could feel it settling around his head until the cushions absorbed the liquid. It started a dreadful warm, and then cooled to decaying room (earthly) temperature. The smell hung heavy still, adding to the toxic concoction that was slowly choking him.

With no watch or phone, Jerimiah could not tell how much time had elapsed since he came to. He felt, however, that it had been several minutes, ten, maybe twenty. How was he still alive, or conscience for that matter? Surely, the conditions and length of time succumbing there to was enough to do him in. Why hadn't he expired? He drifted in and out of senility, losing bits and pieces of time but yet never dying. It was here he lost all track of how long it had been. An hour, two... a day! My God, how could he have survived this long? Jerimiah wrapped on the roof of the coffin with what strength he had left. The efforts vain, he knew, also aware of the effect such labor would have on his psyche. Dashing hope with every knock, the results became that much clearer; no one was coming. No one could hear him. He was trapped. Buried alive! *WHY?* He desperately wondered. *Why won't I die?!* The thought of still being alive after all this time not only opened his eyes to something extraordinary, something that no one would ever know about, Jerimiah knew it was grim torture that he would be buried alive, forever!

THE EMPTINESS

Breathe... Clear your mind, and focus on your breath.

A much-needed escape from the rigors of her busy life, Kate found her salvation in meditation many years ago and has seldom gone a day without a time to clear her head. However, recent feelings of vulnerability have begun to evoke reservations about sitting herself in a quiet room. She couldn't put many of her concerns into words much less share them with her boyfriend.

Even though he was supportive of her beliefs, John was never quite able to grasp the concept of Kate's commitment to her introspection. As the days passed, she wondered how she could begin to describe her feelings to someone who didn't understand the very foundation from which they came. Even once John had accepted everything he remained indifferent, but he recognized the profound effects it held for Kate.

It was meant as a time of reflection, rather a time for purging one's cluttered feelings from the day. To organize and process her thoughts however, for some time, Kate had silently waded in muddled dread. A feeling of impendent, not of any conscious awareness; no physical threat she could speak of. But it was real—as real as anyone could claim. Its presence was not restricted to these moments, as it had begun to invade all avenues of her life. But now, as she sat in silence, her open and receptive mind only brought tension and fear. She tried to give it a name, an image, albeit a misinterpreted one—the emptiness.

Kate continued her routine as she had, despite her apprehensions; she still held a sense of calm. A part of her had already... surrendered.

Kate came into the bedroom and closed the door. Should John come in while she was in practice, he'd understand, and wait.

With the lights turned off, Kate lit a scented candle and sat on the floor, taking in a slow breath before closing her eyes. Thus began her purge of tension, breathing slowly, and becoming lost in the white noise of the night.

The candle, the only assault on the darkness, flickered as a gust of wind came through the window. It brushed alongside her, and she could feel the tiny hairs on her arm, little antenna, stand on end. Kate opened her eyes, and immediately locked her focus on the window. There was nothing. Her mouth slightly agape and her breath turned shallow, as her heart raced and her muscles tensed. After a few seconds, Kate relaxed, and stretched herself out, reaching her arms out wide, getting a feel for the better energies around her. As the calm settled in, her heart beat heavily in her chest as a morbid reminder, but soon, all was quiet.

It began with the filtering of all ambient noise, allowing each to pass through uninterrupted; to try to consciously ignore the outside. This became the first and most difficult practice to understand. Even now, with the breeze coming through the window, like a soft panting breath, Kate relaxed.

Breath, breath…

With breathing calmed, and muscles now relaxed, she had awareness, a sense of openness and surrealism. A clarity that had no definitive definition yet could be easily understood—felt. Yes—that was the only authentic way of explaining it to someone, a feeling of acceptance, of willingness: an absolute vulnerability. Perhaps that was the reasoning… The "why" they came to her, and what she had been searching for.

Kate let out a long relaxing breath.

And like all contemplation, it had indeed called attention to it—the emptiness. There it was, as those times before; nothing, at least nothing of reason. A… thing, the best descriptor she could assign it, which moved within the void of her consciousness. She tried not to focus on it, but the more she tried to avoid it, the more curious it seemed of her. It started as it had before, like a weightless shadow, an emptiness that would move by like a storm cloud in her mind. She thought nothing more of it than this, at first. However, like her last encounter, it had developed further in manifestation, showing more of itself to Kate.

Stay open, stay calm… breath…

The cloud had moved its way closer, disrupting her clarity with its murky presence. It moved in front of Kate's eye with deliberate intent, now with a more lurching gate. It evolved before her, or had it been this way all along. Was it only she who could now hold a greater sense of what this was, she did not know. But it was there, now showing form. She could not tell what it was, but defined shoulders and legs... and a head had become discernable. Kate doubted her own senses, as our minds are programmed to recognize familiarity in that which we cannot understand. Perhaps it was this notion that was giving it shape; a quadruped, moving heavily, as if it were carrying too much weight. However, what she saw next left little room for doubt; nothing she could convince herself of would have catered denial, as it now was showing eyes. Bright yellow beams of light that looked on her like headlights of an oncoming, foreboding truck. They flashed and faded fast, like a blink, an assessment of her presence she might have guessed.

No matter the logic or reason, it provided no comfort or security, and her muscles were no longer relaxed, but tense—imprisoned in dread. The eyes were gone, but it remained there, ominous and looming. She could sense it had an awareness of her, though she could not place its interest. What did it want? It may have been a question to contemplate, but the eyes had reemerged so suddenly, now even closer, the figure itself hadn't moved at all but it felt like had. So close now. Kate could distinctly feel its breath on the nape of her neck, the warm condensation building that she might have called sweat on any other occasion. *This isn't right*. It wasn't enough to feel it but to hear its heaving efforts taking air into its hollow chest cavity and the low resonance of its grumbling roar, like that of a threatened lion warning a nearby intruder. Whatever it was, she could no longer deny its influence.

***

It was uncommon for John to come home late. Coming up the elevator, John's anticipation continued to grow. Taking slow deep breaths, he did what he could to stifle his nervousness. Even as he somewhat curtailed his thoughts, holding his right hand steady against his leg, in a manner guarding the ring box in his pocket. Contemplating his confidence, but not hesitating in his intent. He knew this was the night he would ask Kate to marry him.

The elevator doors opened, and John stepped out. At this point he had no official plan of action, only to make dinner, and wait for the opportune moment. Turning down the hall, John tried calling Kate one more time, hoping she'd be able to open the door for him. The phone rang until it reached her voicemail, and part of him began to wonder if she was even home. Where would she be? And, why not tell him knowing they had plans made for the evening? John began to sweat a bit, tensing the muscles in his neck and fidgeting all about. But John put his angst aside, now coming to their door. He listened in for a second and could hear

Kate's movements. Grateful she was home, John relaxed his shoulders and produced his keys. He fumbled for a moment between his jacket and his bag, feeling that-*What was that?* John froze, hearing a subtle grumbling sound, like something of a growl, if he didn't know any better.

"Kate?" John inquired curiously. He knocked twice, announcing himself again, "Babe?"

Before he could get his keys into the lock, something barked. He stopped, listening close. *Kate wouldn't have gotten a dog without telling me,* he thought. Then, what...

The door burst into splinters, knocking John aggressively back against the wall. Near unconsciousness, John rolled away from the debris, and what he thought to be the cause. His vision blurry and his head throbbing, bleeding from a gash in his forehead, he did not notice the creature approach him.

Its heavy, gnarled paw stomped next to John's head, taking in hoarse breaths like that of a predator looming over its prey, waiting for its opportunity to pounce. It remained so still, observing, and dominantly postured over John.

John turned and finally saw what was looming over him, within an inch of the creature's nose, or what he perceived to be its nose. The pits that seemed to smell the air were long and thin, and ran about two inches vertical up its skull. Its head was shaped like an oversized football. Its skin dark and charred looking, though it shimmered in the light. Its features resembled that of a rock face, muscular and rough. He could see no eyes and only deep crevasses where ears might be. Its neck looked to line up with its back as it leaned in closer moving John back against the wall. It postured like a cat ready to pounce, and John notices two protrusions, what he could only interpret as horns, coming out from its shoulder blades; they seemed to rise in an aggressive stance.

John tried to look away, but a small glint of light caught his attention. Hanging from the creature's neck was a familiar piece of jewelry, the diamond heart necklace he had given… *Kate?*

Cautiously, he reached under the creature's chin and held the heart in his palm. The creature didn't seem to react; indeed, it was not an illusion. It was the very same necklace John had bought Kate for Christmas the year before. He looked on the creature—his girlfriend—with a sense of dread and desperation. *What had happened to her?*

John rose to an elbow to face her, when a sudden sharp scream came from down the hall. John turned, as did Kate, both looking over at a young girl in her pajamas standing at her door, screaming in terror. Their neighbors, the girl's parents had now emerged to see for themselves, and they both gasped at the sight, as well, hauling their daughter back inside.

The commotion and the screams drew attention from other neighbors who had begun to line the hall. Murmurs waved through the hall over the creatures growing agitation.

Its posture, now more aggressive; its head lowered under poised shoulders, ready to pounce, with a deep groan building within its chest.

John brought himself up onto a knee, looking around but not knowing in the slightest what to say or how to react. He could sense the creatures—Kate's—anxiety, as it she backed up a few steps. The distance was growing, as she spun and faced the opposite end of the hall where John had come from.

As even more eyes fell on the situation, John saw that Kate was crouched, and a subtle grumbling roar was building in her chest. There was no time to warn or even react, as the creature lunged forward, nearly clearing the length of the hall with a single stride.

The onlookers fell back against their doors and into their apartments. However, none were able to close their doors before the creature passed by them again.

John watched in shock, as did all remaining eyes, while the creature—Kate—cleared the rest of the distance by scaling the walls and the ceiling in a spiraling manner until it reached the adjacent window. Without any sort of pause or hesitation; no concern for the impending fall, it crashed through the window and was lost to the night.

There were no sounds of impact, no screams, no indication it had fallen the six stories to the concrete alley below, but it—Kate—was gone.

John remained on the floor among the pile of shattered debris, held at an odd position on one leg leaning on his opposite hand. His free hand still held out to his side, clutching the necklace he gave to his girlfriend. It dangled for a moment until he brought it in front of him, his eyes fixed on the enticing glisten of the diamond pendant, and the shimmering shards of glass that remained desperately clung to the window frame. His world, in a way, had quite literally come crashing down around him. Still, he couldn't help but wonder where she was going.

THE MORE YOU GNOME

Norm and Kay stood outside a beautiful home, as beautiful as potential can promise. It was in an obvious need of repair, which explained the bargain offer. Indeed, for their first home, they couldn't refuse. However, their optimism was not without caution, especially when presented against the backdrop of a dog's decayed body found in the upstairs bedroom during their tour, along with the realtor's endless apologies for the grotesque sight. Norm and Kay Waldwick were not without their hesitation, especially since their seven-year-old daughter, Danni, was the one who discovered the scene. Kay was quick to move Danni outside, leaving Noah with the realtor, Judy.

"I am profoundly sorry, Mr. Waldwick," Judy stated, following Noah down the stairs. "We did an inspection two days ago, and there was no sign of the animal, or any other disturbances then."

Noah didn't want to listen to anymore at the moment, exiting the house and approaching Kay and his daughter, who seemed much calmer. This, in turn, made Noah calmer, enough so he could address Judy, who was waiting on the porch. She stood patiently; her embarrassment was shown in her stiff posture, concerned about Danni but knew enough to stay out of the way for now.

Amidst the muddled conversation, Kay and Danni ventured off into the yard, observing the foliage. The flora was impressive. Thick and lustrous, it hid away the road and any invading noises therein. The smells were vibrant, almost tactile in essence, excited with life. Very potent, intoxicating even, Kay noticed. Though pleasant, it was overwhelming, but Danni didn't seem bothered at all. In fact, Kay noticed her daughter's attitude shift dramatically. Soon after, Danni became visibly more energetic and began to frolic about the yard, like a character out of a fairytale.

Judy's shoulders relaxed a bit, as Noah turned to address her. The gruesomeness of the image was still very fresh in his mind, but he managed to maintain his composure.

"I can't tell you enough how sorry I am," Judy began remorsefully.

"She'll be fine," Noah said passively.

To Judy's surprise, they continued talks about the house. And, as hard as she found it to ignore the previous situation, the tour continued, albeit a verbal one. They had seen enough of the house, in the visceral view of one of the bedrooms upstairs. Judy described the other as a mirrored image, purposely keeping the descriptive notes quick and pithy. It seemed to work as she moved on to the basement, which she described as spacious and near finished. The walls were a solid concrete foundation, though the ceiling was incomplete with exposed wires and insulation. Noah gave an acknowledging nod, as Judy now remembered she hadn't been downstairs for some time either. Her heart skipped a beat, thinking on what, if anything might be down there. *Another animal, or God forbid, a body?* The thought had involuntarily flickered in her head, as ridiculous as it was. When was the last time she had been down there? She swallowed her dread and finished up the conversation on what she felt to be a relatively positive note.

They parted ways; while Noah met Kay and Danni under the willow tree in the back yard, Judy moved to wait by her car. As much as Noah didn't want to bring it up, as it looked that Danni had all but forgotten about it already, he asked Kay how she was feeling.

"She seems okay." Kay said with an inflection, which was more than Kay could say about herself.

Noah knew how much she liked this place from the start, and could see the struggle in Kay's eyes now wanting to walk away, but unable to do so. And for a brief moment, Noah was able to picture his wife's regret should they turn the house away. "Are you okay?" Noah asked with a leading concern.

Kay turned her gaze up to Noah, examining him as well as her own thoughts. She stood and took a breath before being able to look at the house again. It was here Noah could see the gears turning, and the puppy dog look, *that's not helping matters,* glaze back into her eyes.

It was an alluring place, apart from the obvious; a true fixer-upper but nothing outside Noah's ability. The more prominent feature that stood out was the lush foliage and richly vibrant gardens that occupied most of the yard. Strangely contrast to the structures neglected condition; it made the house seem like an afterthought, dropped onto a foreign world.

Judy came to attention as Noah rejoined her by her car.

"I think we're going to need a few days to think it over some more," Noah informed her.

"I completely understand, Mr. Waldwick," Judy acknowledged. "If you'd like, I can look into any number of other properties of the like, and maybe we can..."

Judy paused, noticing Kay approaching. Noah turned to see his wife. "Mrs. Waldwick. I was just informing your husband that I would take a look and see what else was available for your requirements."

Kay turned to Noah, "I think we can make it work here," she said quietly, though Judy's brightened expression suggested she heard Kay's comment.

"You sure?" Noah confirmed.

They both looked back to Danni, still running through the yard, happy as can be. The incident, as far as they could tell, had been forgotten for her. They looked at each other, as Kay showed a half-grin. Noah also, as they looked back to

Danni, who was running around the side of the house, out of view.

"Danni!" Kay called out, running after her.

Noah turned back to Judy and smiled. "I guess we'll be taking it," he sighed.

A decision Judy was happy to hear, as she was equally surprised, and relieved. Not to say she wasn't happy for them, she still couldn't help but feel as though she were leaving them with a tainted home.

It was not the first instance of macabre ruin to befall the property, though it was the only of its kind to be physical in nature. There were other rumors, though. People seemed to have a general unease about the place, but for no discernible reason. Some went out of their way to avoid its presence. It didn't matter now; the Waldwick's looked at these claims as they were: rumors.

They took their place, and were moved in a few weeks later. Their anticipations were great; however, the image of the mutilated dog lingered in their minds. It may only have been the initial jitters; the first nights in a new house are almost always difficult, with every creak and groan of the structure worthy of suspicion. It made for some uneasy nights at first, and needless to say. Noah and Kay had dedicated the unspoken room to a storage area for the time being. It was still somewhat unsettling when the thought occurred to either of them, or when they had to go in there to retrieve something, but it was noticeably fading away as time passed.

During the last few months, the family had done well with settling into their new home. And while Danni anticipated a new year in a new school, Noah and Kay had slowly started to get acquainted with their neighbors. The first they encountered was Tom Harris, an elderly widower of about his late seventies, who had been living in the house next door for more than thirty years.

Tom was happy to finally see new and kind people living next door once again. Among the notations of the area's layout, points of interest, and places to avoid, he seemed to be rather mum as to any question given about the home itself. His answers were simple and nondescript, as if he were trying hard to avoid any conversation about it.

"It's been empty for a time," Tom commented. "I remember the last couple had left rather quickly. We never got a chance to wish them well."

As Tom spoke, Noah and Kay had picked up on his curious eye, shifting periodically to their house. His posture stiffened and shifted from side to side. As open as he was before, Tom now held his hands in his pockets, as not to reveal his fidgeting hands. It didn't consciously register with either of them at the moment, but later that night, after putting Danni to bed, Kay had mentioned her feelings to Noah.

"Did you notice anything odd about Tom earlier?"

"Like what?" Noah had forgotten.

Kay had thought about it again. If Noah genuinely did not remember anything about it, then maybe she was overthinking it. She dismissed her question, and they settled down for the night. It had been their first real quiet night together since they moved in. While boxes still littered the house, for the most part things were as they should be. It was a moment they couldn't pass up on each other, and thus became an evening of thriving intimacy.

Their throws were passionate and lustful as if they hadn't seen each other like this for a lifetime. In many respects, it had felt that way for them. Their love was ensconcing, and for that reason, they didn't notice the shifting in the closet door. It hung very loose on the track; one of the many projects Noah had to tend to, jittering to a degree, as if something were lightly bumping into it from the inside.

Kay heard the commotion and halted Noah to listen. Her body tensed, but nothing seemed to happen. The pair waited, and eventually, Kay started to relax, but on sooner had she calmed down, did a box fall from the top shelf, sending its contents crashing to the closet floor. The pair jolted out of bed, scrambling to get the lights turned on.

The box held various small knickknacks, which were now spread out across the floor. Approaching it, Noah stepped forward and opened the closet door. He examined the scene, and found a dislodged ceiling panel. His first thought was a raccoon or something of the like. Noah reached to pull the panel closed. Kneeling down, Noah gathered up everything back into the box, and set it aside to deal with later.

Still trying to catch her breath, Kay made her way to their dresser for a shirt. While throwing on her clothes, she heard a kind of scratching from inside the walls. It sounded too real, even seemed to move. Kay opened the bedroom door and slowly stepped out.

Their cat Shaggy, greeted her, brushing his body against her legs. It felt deliberate, as if the cat was trying to get her attention. But then the cat moved away and focused on the wall. He followed the sound along the ground molding and ambled out of sight.

The scratching returned, louder than ever, and then Kay heard someone groan. She stepped out and saw Danni standing at the rail above.

Kay exhaled a sigh of relief, "Danni, what are you doing up?"

"I couldn't sleep. Something woke me up upstairs," Danni said groggily.

Kay headed upstairs while Noah inspected the closet again. He stood silent, listening. He didn't mind the scurrying thing, so long as it stayed up there. He turned to leave, but halted again when the "something" scratched within the wall. The noise inflicted a nervous tension he would feel for the rest of the night. Not that he was scared, he'd never admit that, but the disturbing annoyance of not knowing what was happening, what damage was being done, and the fact that he'd have to wait to find all this out was unsettling enough.

Kay laid Danni back down to bed. It hadn't been the crash that woke her up as Kay had originally thought, but something else. "They're scratching in my room," she said in a mousy voice. She didn't seem afraid of it, only reporting the matter to her mother.

"It's alright, honey," Kay assured her, plainly. "Your father will take care of everything tomorrow." Kay tucked her in.

"They don't want to be bothered," Danni said innocently enough.

It didn't register with Kay then, as the question came almost out of motherly instinct. "Who doesn't?"

"I don't know," Danni said. "But I can hear them talking, and scratching."

This time, Kay paused as a ripple of fear moved down her chest and settled in her stomach. A ridiculous reaction, she felt, but she couldn't shake it. "I think you should just try to get some sleep, okay?" Kay suggested. Danni settled in and rolled over as Kay stood. She took a step toward the door and turned off the light; not before looking back across the walls of the room, listening for anything strange, did she close the door.

For the next few weeks, things were quiet. Kay had even found the time to tend to the garden. It was a weekend for the three of them to set up their own space, an advantage they all took. Danni was busy putting her room together, while Noah had left to run some errands, leaving Kay to her business, waiting on the exterminator.

It wasn't listed as any kind of attribute when they were buying the house, but the gardens were nothing short of incredible, supernatural even. And despite her confident green thumb, Kay felt a measure of guilt in preparing to defile what looked to be something special on its own. Bright green shrubs, almost fluorescent looking, plotted each corner garnished with white and blue flowerings that looked like lilac stems, but it was nothing of what Kay was familiar with. Rich roses of the deepest red she had ever laid eyes on spidered up the trestle and fanned out to almost completely cover the entire east wall of the garage, as if it were a hand of green tentacles slowly taking hold of the house. A path cut through the thicket led to a faded, cracked concrete birdbath that lay on its side, forgotten. Likewise, was the bench where the path ended; broken and falling to pieces, held together barely by its metal frame.

Kay took slow, tentative steps through the thick brush, exploring the confined area and, while standing at the center, she lost sight of the surrounding yard and neighborhood. It was amazing; she remembered the feeling of how she could be lost in her own yard, not two feet from the porch. If not for the proximity to the house, she may have lost sight of it as well.

This wasn't the day of tending; it was a time to explore and discover. She extended her arms and ran them through the dew-covered leaves, finding that it wasn't exactly a wet covering, but more of a sap-like fluid that gave her hands a tacky feel. *It was indeed bizarre*, she thought, examining the leaves closer, then her hands. It didn't seem to burn or stain in any way, but she was captivated still.

As Kay turned back to the house, wanting to wash the sap from her hands, she noticed something even more out of place. Tucked under the shrubbery, rooted at the base of every plant, were small clusters of mushrooms. Some of the heads were cut with precision, too clean to have been eaten, or knocked off. As with everything else, Kay could not identify their species, but could only liken them to that of a cartoon; brightly colored, obscenely so, and spotted, dripping what looked to be the same sappy substance. It was a foggy colored fluid that hung thick drips suspended just before separation.

Kay knelt down, tempted to touch her findings, but a knot in her throat made her hesitate. As strange as they were, they looked artificial, like melting plastic. A stick lay next to her foot, and Kay used it to prod at the head and stems until a few knocked free. She moved closer but was halted by chittering whispers from under the porch. Her eyes fixed on the broken section of the lattice; from the darkness the hushed chirping continued. She could see nothing. After a few moments the sounds seemed to dissipate. Turning back to the mushrooms, Kay skewered two of the caps and brought them up to the light. *Strange*—in the sunlight, they glistened like crystal—*beautiful*, she thought. Her interest peaked; Kay turned to take them inside to do some homework on them later.

Coming out to the walkway, Kay met the exterminator as he was pulling into the driveway. While she waited, a sudden rustling swept behind her, like that of a small animal suddenly running off. There was no time for her to investigate as the exterminator approached.

"How are you?" He extended his hand. "Mark Allen."

Danni came to her window which overlooked the front yard and part of the driveway. She saw her mother walking toward the truck, talking friendly to the exterminator. Danni looked on with mild curiosity, until her attention was drawn to Shaggy who was frantically scratching at the wall by her bed.

Danni approached the cat, "What you doing, kitty?"

Danni stood above Shaggy, waiting for a response of some kind. The cat seemed disinterested, or unaware of Danni's presence, continuing to scurry around her feet as if it were tracking something in the wall, scratching and sniffing.

Danni picked him up, and continually had to readjust to Shaggy's wormy protest. She didn't know why he was so excited, but soon found herself staring at the wall, as well. Leaning in closer, she could hear the slight scurrying about on the other side. It seemed to go on for several seconds until it stopped abruptly.

Shaggy, then hissed violently.

Back outside, Kay introduced herself to Mark. "I think they know you're here," she said with a mild chuckle. "I just heard something run off under the porch, there."

Mark gave a half-grin and turned back to his van. Kay waited until he was out of view. She could hear Mark gathering up his gear at his van, as she then looked down at the planking of the porch. Kay scuffed her foot a bit to agitate what might be under there. If it were an animal, she preferred it to run away, rather than suffer at the hands of someone who was here to kill it. There was no sound, but Kay stopped at her door when she noticed Tom by his fence, watching Mark's progress with some curiosity.

Tom saw Kay coming over and saw her see him; it was too late for him to leave.

As she approached, Kay could see the concern in Tom's expression, as he watched Mark unload.

"How are you, Tom?" Kay started.

As he continued to watch Mark work, he said, "You, uh, got something going on there?" His tone shifted; there was doubt, now, in his question.

Kay had told Tom about the odd occurrences that had been going on lately, that an invading raccoon might be responsible for everything. Tom didn't offer anything further on the matter, but Kay could clearly see the doubt on his face.

"Do you know what happened to the other people who lived here?" Kay asked. "Why they left?"

"No, they seemed perfectly happy," Tom said. "Then one day they were just gone." He went on to tell Kay how the previous residents may have been victims of a robbery, which is what may have led to their abrupt departure. They were a very well-to-do couple, not so lavish in their standings except for a prominent pearl necklace the woman would wear daily. "I had never seen her without it on," Tom said. "Perhaps it held a certain sentimental value."

For some reason, the image of the dog's body had burst into Kay's mind, and she told Tom about that incident. There was no connection he could figure, but Kay could tell that he was even tenser from the revelation.

"You seem like very nice people, and I don't want to cause you any undue stress," Tom continued, "but if I were you, I'd leave." Kay looked bothered, a bit frightened even. "That house has been nothing but trouble for anyone living there." He made it sound like it was cursed somehow. That in some way no one could settle down in it.

For the time, Kay happened to agree, but she didn't know what to make of Tom's comments. As much as she wanted to write it off as the ramblings of an old man, he seemed too genuine to do so, and Kay and Tom parted ways.

Walking passed Mark, who was now shoulder deep in the hole under the porch, Kay headed back in the house. Tom's words had stuck with her, and she couldn't help the sensation that something was wrong with the house itself. But she shelved this away, as the over activity of her mind. The situation would have driven her crazy; Kay moved back inside.

It had been nearly two hours, and Kay was lost in her chores, not noticing the fading daylight outside. She caught a slight chill, and only when Noah had finally come home did she start to close the blinds.

As Kay continued to go about her business in the kitchen, Noah got himself a drink of water and stood out of her way. He looked around the area, after noticing he hadn't seen their daughter in sometime.

"Danni upstairs?" he asked.

"Yeah, I have to check on her in a minute."

Noah walked over to the front window. He glanced down at the cat's food dish, "I guess the cat's up there, too." He looked outside to check on the exterminator's progress.

"Has he found anything yet?" Noah asked Kay of the exterminator.

Kay's mind sparked, she had completely forgotten he was there. She told Noah it had been a while, and they both headed outside to check on Mark's progress.

Noah had noticed the exterminators van on his return home. He hadn't thought anything of it and left the man to his business. Now, coming back out, Noah hadn't understood why neither of them acknowledged the other. Kay stayed on the porch, staying out of the way, watching from above.

"How you doing?" Noah announced in a friendly manner. There was no response, not even any sort of movement from him, or the light. Noah tried again, "Hello?"

No response. Noah and Kay looked to each other, troubled, and Kay's worry grew as Noah stepped closer. He announced himself again, and again, there was nothing. Noah thought humorously that the man had fallen asleep, but as Noah leaned closer, the sight was anything but funny.

Noah grabbed the exterminator's arm, but Mark didn't react. "Hey!" Noah called out. The man's body rolled over, and Noah fell backwards. The partial gleam from the flashlight gave way to Mark's lifeless body; his right arm nearly chewed clean to the bone, as was his shoulder and half his face. There was a stagnant pool of coagulating blood under his body. He could only have been like this for a couple of hours, which meant that whatever had done this was close, perhaps in the house.

Kay's breathing quickened when Noah scrambled to his feet and stumbled out of the brush. "Inside! Inside, now!" Noah screamed at her, waving her back to the door. Kay hurried to meet him there and they ran inside.

While Kay ran into the kitchen, Noah slammed the door shut and ran to the phone. "What is it?!" Kay called out.

Noah grabbed the phone, "When's the last time you spoke to the guy?" Noah frantically asked Kay.

"I don't know," Kay answered, her concern rising, "maybe a couple of hours."

He continued to wait on the phone. Noah told her that the man was dead without any detail. Kay gasped and leaned back against the counter as Noah managed to get a hold of the police. While they waited for what felt like all night, they continued to try and piece together what may have happened.

"Oh, my God," Kay said under her breath.

"You don't remember hearing or seeing anything?" Noah asked with some assertion. Not anger, although it may have come off that way.

Kay had to think a minute, as the memory sank in, "Danni was complaining about something a few nights ago." She thought about it a bit more. "But, she didn't mention anything about what it was." Then it hit her, "I have to go get her!" kay took a stride away to retrieve Danni before Noah stopped her.

"Wait, relax." Noah rebutted, "I don't want her to have to deal with another... body."

Kay leaned against the counter again, bringing her hands together at her lips. The sentiment was clear, and agreed. Though Danni handled the dog's carcass fairly well, this might be too much for her to take in.

In the time left waiting, Kay had told Noah about what Tom had said, that the house was somehow cursed. Noah shot a look of doubt her way. The comment was nonsensical. He leaned back against the counter to catch his breath, leaving Kay to ponder their situation. As hard as they tried not to think of the body lying outside the kitchen window, there was no way for casual behavior to pry the image from their minds.

The stress became overwhelming, and Kay finally broke, "I can't stay here anymore."

Noah took a second to absorb the tired expression on Kay's face, her eyes near to tears. He could barely restrain his frustration, hanging his head. "Not now, okay." Kay's eyes remained fixed on him. He let out a slow hiss of breath before responding, "You know, I would've easily walked away after what we saw coming into this place." Though she never asked, he took the initiative knowing Kay had her heart set. Who was to blame her, really? It wasn't a game they wanted to take part in. It was no one's fault for the dog; it was no one's fault for the night's noises. And unless Kay was holding back a secret, it certainly was no one's fault for the situation waiting outside.

God, what is taking so long? What to do when waiting for a body to be retrieved? Noah couldn't help but chuckle as the thought ran through his head. Each second passed with an audible thump in their ears. But there was something else that caught their attention. There it was again; a sort of tinkering sound they couldn't discern, but it was close by. They may not have caught it if it ended there, but again...

Both shot their eyes at the same closed cabinet; something was running past the dishes. Kay stepped back, as Noah extended his arm toward the cabinet handle, then stopped. Nearby, a box was tucked into the corner still waiting to be unpacked; in it were several pots and pans. Noah reached for a small, but heavy sauce pot, feeling ridiculously doing so, like some 1950's cartoon housewife preparing for an encounter with a mouse.

He swung the cabinet open and saw nothing but toppled and dislodged dishes. Once again, the scurrying sounds persisted, and Noah opened the next door...

The cupboard door at Kay's ankle slowly opened, unbeknownst to her. A sudden sharp pain grabbed her attention; she screamed! Noah spun around to find Kay on the floor, clutching at her calf; a small but vicious piece of flesh had been ripped away. She gripped it tightly as blood flowed freely and through her fingers.

"What the hell?!" Noah bellowed over his wife's cries.

Soon they were overtaken by the sudden eruption of cabinet doors flying open. To their terrified bewilderment, Noah and Kay found themselves quickly overrun by the creatures! Many of them shrieked piercing cries sending chills through their bones.

They bumbled from the cabinet shelves, many of them falling out of sight, pushing each other out, only adding to the growing dread. Their pointed red crowns moved in unison, like a chaotic concert line marching forward. Noah was beside himself, as he quickly tried to get Kay to her feet, not noticing the two little demon gnomes closing in from beneath the kitchen island. Their penetrating screeches caught Noah's attention. He kicked the cabinet door shut, holding it closed against the otherwise innocent stone figures.

But holding them back did little to help their situation. What felt like dozens of the retched creatures, were ferociously beating against the door. He was only one man and didn't know how long he could last against the onslaught.

Unaware of her husband's predicament, Kay limped towards the front door, stopping to turn back, when she realized he wasn't behind her. Noah faced off with the growing numbers which continued to spill out from the cabinets.

"Come on!" Kay screamed to Noah.

Neither of them had the first thought on what they were dealing with. It became all too bizarre. And to think, it had been Danni who presumably saw these things first; that she was that close to such terror. Kay could not help but put Danni in Mark's place outside, seeing her lying in the dirt half-eaten. Then, the thought hit her, "Oh, shit!" Kay scrambled and ran up the stairs after their daughter.

Coming to the base of the stairs, Kay looked up to see Danni standing at the landing, looking down with a look of concern. She wasn't overly frightened, but Danni could hear the commotion, and saw that her mother was hurt.

"Danni, honey, come down here, quick." Kay waved her down, trying to sound as calm as she could.

"What's going on?" Danni voice was raised a few octaves; her mild fear beginning to show.

As Kay hobbled up the stairs, Noah's stammers of confusion as he fended off the little demons, kicking several aside as they closed in on him, rang in her ears. But there was nothing she could do. Coming now within reach of her daughter, Kay took Danni by the arm, trying to hide her need for support. "It's nothing, honey." Kay didn't sound so convincing, "We just need to leave for a bit." Kay would have continued to offer reassuring words, but their effect would have been muted by the sudden crash heard from the kitchen. Kay and Danni looked down the stairs in horror.

Noah rammed his body against the door. The gnomes thumped against the walls and cabinets, only to right themselves back up and scurry out of sight. Noah's eyes darted from side to side, trying to keep track of them. By the sink, a sound of shattered glass caught his attention. Three gnomes fighting amongst themselves over the mushroom caps that Kay had collected. They had destroyed the glass jar and were pushing each other down aggressively to get them.

Noah was confused, but the explanation for the onslaught became apparent. Noah grabbed a nearby ceramic dish and pitched it at the three at the sink. The dish shattered on impact, knocking two of them to the floor.

"Come on, we have to go." Kay hurried Danni along.

"Wait," Dannie objected, "the cat's in my room."

Kay scoffed, but obliged, and pulled herself up, and into Danni's bedroom. She practically fell into the door when opening it.

It was almost quiet in here, as Kay flipped on the light. Danni stayed close behind. Kay scanned the room quickly for any signs of Shaggy. He wasn't anywhere to be seen. "Honey, I don't see..."

"He's under the bed." Danni said excitedly, moving to show her mother.

Kay held her back, and locked her eyes on the underside of the bed. She fell to the floor to inspect more closely, cautious of anything that didn't belong. Kay crawled around Danni's belongings, pushing them aside aggressively, until she found Shaggy cowering in the far corner. He was hiding behind a clear plastic bin, afraid even of Kay.

"Oh, come on, baby," Kay beckoned, reaching as far under as she could. The cat wasn't moved, at all. *This isn't working*. Kay, then, got an idea, and shoved the bin into the corner, flushing the cat out. Shaggy was not happy, but he darted out toward Kay. She tried to catch him, but the cat ran into Danni's waiting arms. "Okay, let's get downstairs."

Kay struggled to get to her feet, unaware of the looming company that was emerging from under the other side of the bed. Only when Shaggy had hissed violently, did she realize she was surrounded by six, or seven gnomes, all with glowing eyes fixed on her wounded leg.

Danni let out a piercing scream, and before kay could react several gnomes locked on to her with sharpened teeth and clawed hands. They crawled up her legs, one of which was profoundly interested in her wound.

Kay screamed, and fell to the floor, as the gnome picked at it curiously, like a child poking at a plate of food. "Get downstairs, Danni!" Kay yelled, "GO!" Kay thrashed, and rolled on the floor, as if she were on fire.

Kay threw away all hesitation. She tore the one from her leg, peeling away another small piece of flesh it was clutching, and threw it against the wall. The force was such that the gnome shattered like glass, leaving a large blue-splatter blotch of "blood" behind. She managed to scatter the rest away long enough for her to crawl back to the stairs.

Behind her, the horrible creatures continued their pursuit, until she slammed the door trapping them inside. She heaved a breath, listening to the commotion within, and the chaos downstairs.

Walking down the stairs, she leaned against the wall, holding firm to the banister. Below, Danni was waiting, clutching the cat with dear life. Kay stepped slowly down the stairs; her ear pressed against the wall, expecting to hear something, and was not disappointed. Scratching tickled the inside of the wall. Then came biting, and cracking. She leaned away in disbelief, and then the drywall fractured. The red-pointed crowns of the creatures pushed through like crude drill heads that made the wall come to life. A dark viscous fluid ran down the jagged parts of sheet rock and wood, as if the wall itself were bleeding, or perhaps from the gnomes gashing themselves on the hardened edges. Kay came to her feet and tripped the rest of the way down. She moved Danni to the door.

In the kitchen, the gnomes' screeching overwhelmed Noah, as another wave of them spilled over the island with gnashed teeth shown and advancing. Noah reacted on instinct, swinging the sauce pot as hard as he could. While one managed to drop away, the other gnome was hit and blasted to pieces, sending a thick splatter of blood along the wall. It was a deep blue, almost black in color, found to be oozing from their hungry mouths and eyes, as well.

Despite the gnomes' many numbers, Noah dispatched them as easily as the others. He felt confident enough to stand his ground.

They retreated, seeing pieces of their fallen gnomes along the walls, scattering swiftly back into the cabinets and behind the desks, disappearing from sight in seconds. Other than the destruction left behind, they'd never have known anything strange had happened.

Noah dropped the pot and staggered back toward his waiting wife and daughter. "Move, move," Noah yelled. They guided each other out the door just as the first police unit pulled into their driveway. *What timing!* They hurried to meet the officer.

"Whoa, whoa!" the officer halted them, bringing them to the hood of his car. He could see their distress, as well as Kay's limp, and the odd blue fluid splashed all over Noah. The officer held them there, allowing them to explain the situation. As much as Noah and Kay wanted to express the truth of what just took place, the words didn't make sense in their minds. Their explanation was that of some unidentified animal they did not see, that was also responsible for the exterminator's death.

The officer looked over the house, then back to see his partner now pulling in. As the second officer approached, he remained with the family while his partner investigated the body.

"No! No, don't go near it," Kay pleaded.

The second officer turned back at their warning, curious, but alert. A sudden screech brought his attention back to the porches rail, where yet another gnome had jumped up. The officer stumbled back, as the creature gnashed its teeth, soon joined by another dozen lining the porch.

"Shoot'em, shoot'em, goddammit," Noah yelled, tempted to reach for their gun!

Both officers looked on in disbelief, until the gnomes advanced down from the porch and charged the group. They were quick to take Noah's advice, as both officers drew their weapons, and fired at the creatures. Kay quickly huddled over Danni and the cat, trying desperately to hide her daughter from the gunfire. It was a quick and panicked shooting that was over in seconds, but an insanely bizarre moment that would last for years in their minds.

The gunfire was over, leaving the fragmented remains of the gnomes littering the lawn, and their blue entrails painted along the front of the house. The two officers were stunned, silenced by their acts, and more so on what they had just seen. They looked to each other, then to the family, equally perplexed at the absurdity of the situation.

It was nerve-wracking to think what might have happened to them, how they would ever be able to tell their story. Kay, Noah, the officers; they couldn't imagine what to think, especially when they found the body. It took them a few minutes to compose themselves, but upon inspection, there didn't seem to be a body.

Noah, Kay, and the first responding officer all approached and were equally baffled at what they saw. A slight red stain remained on the lattice, and in the dirt, but the body—all traces of it—was gone! The words were choked in all their throats, and their heads racked with the pain of stress. Shaggy continued to struggle in Danni's arms, trilling and fussing. Little did any of them know of the chittering sound in the air, and the dancing yellow orbs that continued to watch from beneath the porch.

THE J.A.R. (Justified Artificial Reality)

Whatever this feeling is, I won't be able to put it into words. The trees, the landscape; that's the pine tree in front of our house! The start of a perfect sunny day is beginning to peek over the horizon, the first sight of it all coming through the window—our window. My God, the spectrum of detail is beyond comprehension, a truly overwhelming experience, to say the least. Oh, the questions, philosophical and practical, how fast they were piling up. So many; they felt as though they were actually gaining mass and weighing my body down. I couldn't recite all my thoughts if I wanted to, but the ever-increasing curiosity was enough for me to know that I wouldn't be sleeping at all tonight.

The image began to move again...

It was like watching a movie; it... He! It was him; it was Philip. He turned to the vanity mirror and I saw his face. I knew I would break out in tears. I just didn't know when. It... He turned around and looked down onto the bed now. Oh, I wish he would've stood there a while longer, but that wasn't Philip. He wasn't one to linger at his own reflection. It's like looking into a window of the past. No, not the past, wrong tense... parallel? A hand reached out on the screen, his hand, coming to rest on a figure in the bed lying under the covers. It moved, and I knew who it was, but nothing could've prepared me for the sight of my disheveled bed-headed image looking back at me. I need to put an end to this... this...

-CLICK-

The snap of the switch was stiff, absorbed by the soundproof walls. The screen overhead turned off, and a moment later, the lights rose to a soft luminous glow. Anna Doyer stood in the center of the room dressed as though she had shown up for a job interview. Braced against a raised podium set forward off-center of the room, she clutched a handkerchief in her right hand. It was pointless now; she had given up wiping away the tears from her face, which continued drawing distorted lines of makeup down her cheeks.

She stood silent, staring through the floor, still trying to absorb and comprehend what she had seen. She looked to the J.A.R. chamber where her husband was, at least part of him. By all accounts, he was dead, yet he continued to exist within a box shelled inside the wall below a wide-screen monitor, fitted into the wall at a slight angle a little above eye level. Through here, Anna could watch her husband's continued existence through his eyes. The cylindrical room, its soft walls, and shallow dome felt like a padded room for anyone that might lose their minds, which Anna wasn't far from entertaining.

A lock snapped from behind and the door opened. Anna straightened up, trying her best to pull herself together as fast as she could. She wiped the tears away from her face and turned to meet the nurse at the door waiting to usher her out.

Until the nurse escorted her down the hall a short distance, through a set of heavy double doors, Anna stood aside.

The nurse waved a badge in front of a sensor, and the locks released. They stepped through, passing several closed doors, no doubt filled with people as befuddled and grief-struck as she was. But Anna was more puzzled now, walking with a blank expression, as she scanned the hall for anyone else with a similar appearance; at least then she wouldn't feel so alone. She was a woman unto her own mystery, until they came to an open door.

"You can have a seat. Dr. Greenwood will be in with you shortly," the nurse said, trying to comfort Anna.

Anna entered slowly, moving cautiously. Were there more bizarre anomalies that awaited her? Hell, after what she had seen, she began to doubt her own senses, her own reality.

"Is there anything I can get you, Mrs. Doyer?" the nurse asked.

Anna stood close to the wall, a couple of steps inside the door jamb the empty area of the room feeling like the safest place. Still trapped in her mind, Anna massaged the handkerchief between her thumb and fore finger; the texture of a familiar surface reminded her that this was real. She was here. But the nurse's question did not register with Anna.

This was a familiar reaction, not the first one to have been stricken like stone, the nurse understood, and left Anna alone, closing the office door.

This was one of the last places Anna and Philip had been; weeks ago in fact, when they had worked up the courage to come. Philip's cancer had progressed aggressively, and neither of them was ready, nor knew how to prepare. And when they found this opportunity they gave up on goodbyes and decided to focus on staying together. It seemed like it had such promise then, but now, after what she had witnessed in the chamber a moment ago, it wasn't comforting in the slightest, going as far as thinking of it as disheartening, ominous even.

Anna tried to compose herself, casually observing the folksy art and the warm decor, but it did very little to calm her nerves. Even the resounding hum of the fish tank in the far corner of the room sent a chilling vibration through her body. This wasn't what she thought it would be. Something was off, and Anna began to wonder if it was her own feelings toward her husband, more specifically the augmented representation of him. Perhaps the fact that Anna couldn't bring herself to refer to Philip as alive, nor could she say he was dead had something to do with it. She had to decide this first before moving forward.

Anna finally managed to spark the nerves in her legs and took a step toward the chair by the desk until the metal door handle rattled. Anna spun around as the door swung open. In walked an aged, but well-groomed gentleman, dawned in the traditional white lab coat with a clipboard tucked under his arm. "Hello, Anna," he said pleasantly, extending his free hand with a smile. His name tag glinted in the thin rays of sunlight—Dr. Alan Greenwood.

"Sorry, I got held up. Our financiers are always checking our progress. Why don't you have a seat?" Dr. Greenwood suggested, circling with purpose to the opposite side of the desk. Anna took it slow, easing into the chair.

"So..." Dr. Greenwood began, letting out a long exhale, "I... imagine you have some questions." Smiling, with a slight chuckle; a poor attempt at light-hearted humor.

Questions... Oh, there's plenty! Anna thought. The tears were still welling, brimming on her eyelids, but the curiosity, confusion rather, was overwhelming. There was so much to discuss, but Anna was speechless. Dr. Greenwood saw this and offered, "How about I start?"

Anna agreed, nodding gently.

"So," Dr. Greenwood continued, "why don't we start with your thoughts, Anna?" He leaned back in his chair, looking now more like a therapist than a medical doctor. "It seems our clients thus far have come to expect one thing, and end up... well, at a loss for words."

That she was. Anna couldn't think of anything to say or ask which compounded her already painful thoughts. This was to be a moment of solace, celebration even, but it was neither. Instead, there was only quiet dismay at a time where

Anna thought she could not feel anymore alone. Being part of such a small group of participants, she had to know she wasn't the only one, "What do they say?"

Dr. Greenwood's description was a general overview of how his clients typically go through stages of grief. Their anticipation, he says, is often from a measure of false expectation, which then turns to confusion, or sometimes shock. "What you're feeling now is perfectly normal, so far as we've come to have on record."

Anna went quiet again, mildly content by Dr. Greenwood's words. Anna hoped she wasn't silently going crazy, which she felt was the next step in her mind.

Dr. Greenwood continued detailing the services and conditions of the program, but for Anna it was muffled beats that pulsed in her ear. Her attention was still back in that room, still trying to make sense of the situation itself. Above all else, more than how she would be able to handle this, how could she absorb all this information, there was the more obvious, and impending question. "Is Philip alive, or dead?"

"Well, in a manner of speaking... both," Dr. Greenwood answered. His attempt at dulling out the hesitation was clear; not that he didn't believe in what he was doing, ethically, or otherwise. Still, it was indeed a stretch of the imagination, even when brought to life (an interesting choice string of words). It seemed that even the professionals couldn't cope with the reality of it all.

Dr. Greenwood made sure to let her know that there were no promises of resurrection, as it were. As far as this world was concerned, Philip Doyer was indeed deceased. His body was dead and buried in a plot two towns over. However, here in this place, in what Philip would now consider *his* world he was very much alive, and unaware of anything else. He had merely awakened from a very deep sleep, and that any concerning thoughts, or doubts he may experience about his existence, were presumably buried so deep in his subconscious he'd never be able to conceive of them with any sort of clarity.

So many vagaries and assurances walking hand in hand. Hell, it wasn't like anyone here could precisely know what was going on in another's mind no matter how wired in they were. But why not? They were able to keep a person—a brain—alive. Why couldn't they control what it knows or doesn't know? It was a lot for Anna to take in.

"What about me?" Anna asked abruptly.

"I'm sorry?" Dr. Greenwood replied curiously.

"I have a contract here, as well. Will I be able to see him when...?" she trailed off.

Dr. Greenwood sighed; he knew where this conversation was heading and felt it best not to venture down such dark alleys. This wasn't someone's deathbed, or funeral, this place had created a whole new stage of dying, one that hadn't been given a name yet:
Denial...

Anger...
Bargaining...
(This...)
Depression...
Acceptance...

"Let's not worry about that now, okay?" He said leaning forward, trying to speak in the most comforting tone possible. Dr. Greenwood explained that at their present stage of development, they were still in their infancy. He explained that soon they would have the means for clients to speak to one another and, ideally yes, as Anna had asked, one day for people to interact with each other on a more intimate scale. He made it clear that the applications for this program were boundless, requiring only time.

"But we can offer something in the meantime," he said in a more positive tone, his posture straightened up. Dr. Greenwood went into his desk and retrieved a file folder. He opened it and turned it to face Anna. She didn't seem too enthusiastic about any more conditions or circumstances. Her mind, it seemed, had been pushed to its limit for the day. Nevertheless, Dr. Greenwood felt this might bring some excitement into an otherwise bleak review. He waited.

Anna reluctantly faced him. She leaned in to read the paper. It was a profile page of her husband with his picture, clipped to the corner. Anna took in a long breath, composing herself before she had a chance to cry.

"This is your copy to keep," Dr. Greenwood began. "Now, on the back page is something that... you're going to have to hear to understand."

Anna was curious, and for the first time, her attention was on something other than her husband's state of being. She focused on what Dr. Greenwood had to say.

Dr. Greenwood pulled the phone closer to him and turned the file his way. "Anna..." he said cautiously, "would you like to talk to Philip?"

Anna looked to him rather confused. *Talk to him?* Somehow, the question of 'how' didn't seem sufficient enough to encompass the entirety of her inquiry. She could see, too, the anticipation in the doctor's expression. Even he was amazed at this leap in ability! She only answered with her already befuddled expression.

Dr. Greenwood tightened his lips into a slight grin and began to dial. Before punching the command to call, he looked to Anna. "You will have a chance to speak. But please remain quiet until I say, okay?" Anna turned slightly to the phone, waiting for what she already knew was coming.

Dr. Greenwood hit the key, and a dial tone hummed over the speaker, followed by a quick succession of punched numbers. The phone rang once, twice... and with each ring, Anna could feel her heart throbbing in her neck, and the blood rushed to her head. Her breath was torn through her throat, and she clasped her hands over her mouth when Philip answered:

"*Hello*?" Philip's voice answered, sounding calm and pleasant.

"Hello, Mr. Doyer, this is Dr. Greenwood of St. Joseph's Memorial. How are you today?" He looked up to see Anna's reaction as Philip responded, which was nothing short of shock, the closest one could get without passing out.

"*Oh, how are you, sir*?" Philip answered. "Good to hear from you finally." Philip chuckled lightly, as did Dr. Greenwood.

"I'm doing well. I have some good news for you, Mr. Doyer. We got the tests back on the mass, and there is no sign of cancer. It is completely benign."

Anna looked up to the doctor. Her expression morphed to utter confusion, instinctively wanting to correct him. Philip did have cancer. It killed him. There was some rather damning evidence in the room down the hall.

"*Oh, God!*" There was a pause, "*I can't tell you how I feel right now.*"

Anna wondered why he would say such a thing, more so, if this was indeed Philip, why was he accepting this as fact. As they continued, her emotions played a tug-of-war between shock and confusion. As much as she wanted to call out to him, she couldn't. Not right now.

"Listen," Dr. Greenwood continued, "I have to go. I just wanted to let you know the good news."

"*Yes, thank you, Doctor!*"

"Why don't you call me with a date that works for you, and we'll schedule a follow-up?" He continued as though he were speaking to any ordinary patient. They concluded their conversation. Anna stared deeply into the speaker once the line went quiet. After a faint click on the other line, Dr. Greenwood looked up with a smile.

Anna could only muster a shudder, "How..."

Dr. Greenwood went on to describe this amazing application of talking to the subjects. He pointed out that their conversations, while existing in real-time to her, would be delivered to Philip at an appropriate time, thus eliminating any chance for continuity errors and rejection of the program. "Think of it," he said, "as a mailman that knows when to deliver the message, even if you don't." Indeed, what would happen if she were to call at a time when her surrogate was there? This was the first thing that made sense to her today. It was a starting point.

There was more, but Anna had reached capacity for the day. She became restless, squirming, and readjusting in her chair until Dr. Greenwood granted her leave. He stood, as did Anna, and came around to guide her to the door. He picked up the file, handing it to Anna before she left. He reminded her that this was hers to keep and that there were instructions for moving forward and numbers (*only one that really mattered to Anna*) for any situation, and not to hesitate to call. She thanked him, and left without another word.

The entire ride back to the hotel was a blur; her energy and attention remained focused on keeping the events of the last twelve hours from wearing her down. It was a lot to take in, but none more so than the sound of her dead husband's voice, not a recording, but a live, active voice. This she could barely comprehend, and perhaps she was not meant to, but the idea of talking to him both excited and worried her. She was too exhausted to venture into the philosophical arguments of the situation, and found herself debating on whether or not she should try to talk to him. Was she even ready for this? The question was hanging on Anna's back all the way to the room, forcing her to stare up at the ceiling with only the glow of her phone illuminating the room as she stared into it, hoping it would decide for her.

Anna stared at the number on her phone until she worked up the nerve to press the call button. It rang several times, during which she tried to think of what to say, how best to act casual. The line picked up, and Philip's voice answered, "Hello?"

Anna went mute, unable to exert any words. Philip's voice again spoke, "Hello? Who is this?" There was a silence for a moment before the line hung up.

It was overwhelming for her to hear his voice again, and she cried silently, her tears slowly running onto the pillow. All she wanted now was sleep, wishing to lie next to her husband once again. Anna put the phone on the nightstand and retrieved a bottle of sleeping pills. She opened them and dumped several into her hand. She took the pills and laid back on the pillow, staring up at the dark ceiling until her mind faded into nothingness.

Buzz-Buzz-Buzz…

Anna's eyes fluttered open. She reached her hand out from under the covers slapping the top of the clock until it went quiet. She didn't remember setting the alarm. Perhaps it was preset from the last tenant, she rationalized, rolling onto her back and letting out a groggy exhale of breath. Staring at the ceiling, Anna laid with heavy sorrow in her eyes, with a knot in her throat. Before the feeling rendered her to tears, Anna threw the covers off and sat up. Strange as it was, part of her felt as though she were still asleep, trapped in a nightmare she couldn't recall, but the feelings of dread and sadness were ever-present, and there was something more, something not of a dream, nor reality, but rather an instinct of déjà vu. Yet the feeling was fleeting, as she stood up and headed for the bathroom.

The more she moved, the more alert she became as her body awoke, the more certain she was that she'd been here before, like a bothersome echo in her mind. This was clear, and Anna made a conscious effort to keep busy. She splashed her face with water and looked up in the mirror. There, in the reflection behind her, stood an imposing figure—a man. Anna turned, but there was no one there. She approached the door and looked around the room for any sign of someone's presence. She did not feel any fear, no sense of intrusion; it was as though some expected company had left without saying goodbye.

Seeing the figure as clear as day standing in the room and now gone (hidden, perhaps), she found herself with a surprising lack of panic. Someone was in her room when she was all alone. She knew she should have a sense of urgency, but there was none. She packed her bag and exited the dimly lit cavern of a room, stopping at the open door, debating to take one last look inside, wondering if the man would be standing there. She didn't and headed to her car.

Stepping out, Anna noticed the strange lack of noise and activity. No birds, no cars, no life of any kind anywhere. It didn't occur to her at first, but she soon noticed that the breeze, the only other active thing, was only gusting in a single direction, brushing along her left side, as if it were deliberate in doing so. She pushed it out of her mind. There was probably a perfectly rational reason why, so she thought nothing further on it and got in her car.

The door shut, and Anna was enclosed in an even more suffocating box, the resounding silence putting a slight pressure in her ears, making her head ache. She massaged her temples and her eyes, coming to a pinch at the bridge of her nose. She started the car and looked up to adjust the mirror; there, she saw the reflection of the same man again sitting in the back seat.

"I know you," Anna said matter-of-factly to herself. Unquestionably, it was a man, but he appeared less alive than she expected, but not really a ghost, more an apparition—a trick of the light. Either scenario was acceptable; all perfectly rational. Maybe someone else in her situation might have felt fear, but not her. She was curious, waiting for him to respond.

He, too, sat there waiting as his image faded in and out of focus. Anna again rubbed her eyes rather aggressively, and looked up again, this time the man was gone.

Anna pulled out and came around the building, through the emptiness of the parking lot. It appeared that the entirety of the landscape was void of life, a detail she hadn't noticed. Stopping at the speedbump before the road, Anna looked left and right, wondering which direction to head. For the moment, home eluded her, until a seemingly deliberate piece of debris blew by. No deviation in its path, blowing from left to right. Anna decided to follow.

The wind blew like a guiding arrow, as if it knew where she had to go. It was a distance down the road, and it became more surreal; there was still no traffic, no activity, nothing. She almost believed the planet was dead... but why? And why was she here? Coming now to a red light—strange that things still seem to function normally—Anna stopped.

Waiting for several minutes, Anna grew impatient. *Why am I stopped?* She wondered. *There's no one here, no cops, nothing to say I can't go.* Still waiting, the debris and brush that seemed to be guiding her way, were gone for now, yet she felt she was heading in the right direction. Anna reclined in her seat, and then looked up at the mirror. *Was he still there?* Slowly, she tilted the mirror to see, but nothing was there. In his place, however, was the sudden urgency to continue, as the light still refused to turn green. Anna took one last look around then drove through, veering around a sudden pothole before fading into the distance.

Anna slowed around the corner; it was home, but it appeared flat, dimensionless. While she recognized the structure itself, it held no evoking memory. It was a foreign place, like she remembered it vividly from a book or magazine. But it was home, this much she knew. She pulled into the driveway and parked next to the walkway leading to the front porch.

Anna stepped out and drifted toward the front of the house in a haze, not exactly knowing what she might find. The question itself had rendered a morbid curiosity in her mind. What couldn't she see? As she continued, there was a hissing sound that drew her attention back. She turned and saw her car was in ruins, impacted along the front and right side, possibly hit by another car or deer. White smoke billowed out in a thin stream, reaching for the sky. The bizarre sight was jarring but didn't dissuade her movement forward.

That feeling of recognizing someone in a crowd, so certain you know who they are, the same familiarity continued to grow within Anna as she began to walk toward the house. Dawn was breaking and soon she would be without the cover of night. As she dragged her feet across the dew-covered lawn, she could feel the cool dampness of the water seeping into her shoes. Coming to the porch, Anna slowed her pace. The pain, once again, radiating all throughout her body; her head and stomach particularly pulsed with discomfort.

Anna put one foot on the first step, leaning against the railing of the porch, waiting for the pain to subside. As it faded, Anna straightened up and raised her head to look up towards the roof of the house. Her heart began to race again; Anna could describe the layout of the house without even needing to look through a window, she could walk through there blindfolded, and yet the truth was she was looking to break in. *Breaking into my own house?*

Anna stepped up onto the porch and approached the door slowly. Part of her was anticipating someone to peel back the blinds, or a car to pull into the driveway. This was where she'd be caught if that was to be the case. Indeed, there was the soft *wooshhh* of an approaching car cutting through the still air; a black pick-up truck. Inside, she panicked, but remained still, frozen in place. The only thing she could think to do was to fiddle in her pocket as if she were searching for her keys. She didn't know what to do if the truck were to pull into the driveway; that would be a decision she would make at the time. She hid behind the tall line of pine bushes, watching with her nerves on end, as the truck took the sharp curve and drove out of sight.

Anna reached for the doorknob, with the feeling lingering still in her nerves that the door would swing open any moment and she would be caught. But she continued, her body operating on autopilot, taking hold of the door handle. It was locked. *No surprise*, she thought, but what felt odd was she knew where the key was, exactly where it was! No thought, or guessing, she reached down and lifted the plastic flower pot. On the base was a strip of masking tape, a hard piece of metal concealed therein. Anna peeled it off and recovered the brass key. She fit the key into the lock, hesitating. The entire process, from her finding the house, to knowing where the spare key was hidden (could've been a lucky guess, but it didn't feel that way) was all muscle memory, something Anna desperately wanted to question. Still, she knew, even if there was an explanation for all this it wouldn't help. It was maddening now, after encouraging the idea.

The handle turned, and Anna pushed the door open cautiously. There was a subtle brushing sound as the base dragged over the doormat. Anna stepped in and surveyed the area, careful not to make a sound. It was dim, cold, quiet. The outside light had yet to reach the farther corners of the house. She took a step to her right, now standing in the doorway to the kitchen. So familiar, not that she'd ever been here before, but it felt like home. A sudden weight of melancholy came over her, her throat and eyes synching up and tears began to well. She was grief-stricken, a sense of loss; she was certain of it. *Grieving for whom*. This contemplation, along with the unease within the house, registered with her almost simultaneously.

Anna crept through the kitchen, running her fingers across the cabinet doors, trying to feel for something, something that might resonate true. The various knickknacks on the counter tops, the fake fruit, the books, and letters, were all too familiar. Anna picked up an unopened letter, a bill; it appeared to be, addressed to Philip Doyer. *Doyer*, she thought. "Philip," Anna whispered. There was something, a flutter of profound Déjà vu that pushed her forward through the fear.

Coming to the opposite side of the kitchen, to the archway that led into the living room, Anna stopped suddenly, called by something silent. She looked up to the ceiling and slid her fingers up the cabinet wall as far as she could reach. Her fingers didn't touch the top, so without concern for any noise that might alert her presence, dragged a nearby barstool over and climbed up. She peered over the lip of the cabinets, looking into the six-inch gap beneath the ceiling. There it was; she knew it as soon as she read the name on the letter, the .22 pistol hidden away. She picked it up with empty confidence, recognizing the gun itself, and was now trying to remember what she needed it for. She came down off the stool.

Anna looked at the weapon resting in her hands, like a found artifact that need only be studied now. She held it at her side, waiting for the appropriate moment; the looming malevolent presence continued to call to her. While rounding the corner into the living room, she observed a bit more; the rustic décor, the warm environment. She felt comfortable, probably more comfortable than she should. This was the first moment she could remember, albeit a fleeting sentiment of being safe and focused. This was a place she could call home.

Anna took a step forward and stopped again, facing an adjacent door across the room. It was in there; whatever she had come here for was behind that door. Anna walked confidently, striding forward until her nose practically touched the door. She felt the cold metal of the gun in her hand, the other on the doorknob as she quietly turned it and pushed the door open. It was here she felt as though she was being driven, motivated by something other than her own decisions. No direction she could've taken from the hospital to here felt right, even hurt to consider anything other than what she was doing now, even though she didn't fully understand yet. Anna tightened her hold around the grip of the gun and stepped in.

The bedroom was typically darker than the rest of the house, perhaps because the blinds were shut tightly, or its location relative to the layout of the house, still there was something different. This room was a world of its own; a hole in existence that somehow she wasn't able to see. Every object was silhouetted against what little light there was. There was nothing she could distinguish, nor did she have to. To her right, a figure lay in bed, obscured by the blanket pulled almost to the headboard. Anna had found what she had come for; all other matters had dissipated. She tried to get a better look at this person, hoping to understand why she was so drawn to them. Standing this close, her hand hovered over the blanket, waiting for the nerve to peel it back. She felt a connection, a longing for whoever this was. Her fingers touched the blanket, and a sudden rush of panic surged through her entire body, followed by an overwhelming feeling of being watched. H*ad I been caught?*

Anna turned quickly, staring at a shadowy figure, standing in the doorway of the bathroom. It was a slender body, feminine, no doubt there. The flowing hair draped over the faint definition of a bosom, and the dainty profile gave that clear impression. Anna was frozen stiff. She tried to breath, but something pulled the air from her lungs. She watched, as the figure stared right back it seemed, as still and ominous as she might have expected. Examining "her" features, the ones she could see, her eyes moved up, down and around the woman's profile, looking for any indication of life. There was none, no movement at all. The woman stood before Anna like emptiness in the space, a sight that reminded Anna of her trip from the hospital. Anna waited, hoping that the image would clear as the billboards and environment had done for her earlier.

There was nothing this time. This—*she* was something different, and Anna was scared again, threatened, even. She couldn't make any words out to provoke a response, something inside her clamped her throat closed, quite literally, so Anna raised the gun. She repositioned it in her hands and paused before actually pointing it at... her.

The woman didn't move, didn't react at all. Anna was puzzled indeed, but not willing to give up her position of dominance. She didn't want to shoot and tried again to speak. This time, she found what she could say, "Who are you?"

There was no response.

Anna looked over her shoulder at the figure lying in bed. He had yet to notice—or react to their activities. "Who is he?" she asked more desperately. "Why are you in my house!?" There was still no response, no reaction. Anna raised the gun with a stiff arm, with all the appearance and intention to fire. It was more of a threatening tactic to garner an answer; anything at this point would suffice. Anna went as far as pulling the hammer back, as close to shooting without actually going through with it. She was terrified.

The woman came to life at the click of the hammer, as if she had flipped a switch. Her limbs extended out like an octopus' tentacles in one abrupt motion. She lunged forward with one long stride, reaching out with both arms with maddening intent. She made no sound in her attack, but Anna was quick to defend. She lost her balance and pulled the trigger as she fell back onto the bed. She fired once—twice—three—and four times, the last two shots almost certainly went astray, as her position at the time was more concentrated on bracing her fall, than taking aim. But the first two had found their mark, or so she hoped.

There was no assault; the woman fell down, as the man shot up in bed, like awakening from a vivid nightmare. Anna lay on her back at his feet; the gun still clutched in her hand. She was staring straight at him, an odd wave of feelings rushing through her, like her mind was trying to remember who he was. A stranger, yes, but a stranger she recognized, whereas *he* seemed to be looking straight through her like she wasn't even there.

"Phi..." the name began falling out over her lips, but Anna wasn't able to say it.

Philip sat upright in bed, still coming down from a shock he couldn't identify. He turned toward the bathroom and jumped out of bed fully alert. Running over, he nearly fell to where the woman had been standing, and started to sob.

He was cradling a figure in his arms, distraught. To her bewilderment, she observed it to be the woman she had shot. Anna now lay alone; there was no sign of any attack.

"Oh, God!" Philip cried out.

Anna's mind began to seize, feeling as though something indescribable had taken hold of her. She could see what was happening, but only as a passenger trapped in her body. Her eyes moved back and forth from Philip and the bathroom's linoleum floor, holding the woman to the empty space next to her.

"Oh, God, Anna!" Philip screamed, his voice muffled in the shoulder of the woman.

Anna!

The name was clear. It echoed in Anna's mind like a bell. It continued to chime in his voice, *Anna... Anna... Anna...* Her muscles tightened, convulsing as she tried desperately to comprehend what was happening. The echo continued ceaselessly *ANNA... ANNA... ANNA...*

Anna managed to put a finger to the trigger as the only clear thought entered her mind. One word: "Philip." Anna looked, and standing beside her once again was the same darkened figure. She fired! The figure before her didn't move this time, Anna had missed. How could she have, with the barrel only inches from the figures frame? She fired once again. This time there was something, a distortion in her vision. The figure standing over her began to glitch, coming in and out of view in fragments, much like a computer would that was overrun with information. It broke apart, then reassembled in places, becoming part of the scene.

"Philip," Anna was finally able to say as if another had used her own voice to remind her. "Philip," she said again, turning to look to him.

Still knelt beside the woman, her limp body held in his arms, Philip turned to look to Anna. His face was emotionless, blank. He continued to look through her like she wasn't there.

Anna observed, noticing the figure in his arms was behaving the same way, fragmenting and dissipating in places. Philip didn't seem to notice. "Philip," Anna managed again, this time with an almost certain memory. She knew him but didn't understand how, or why. "I'm sorry," Anna said under her breath. With a sudden motion, as if being maneuvered by some outside force, she pointed the gun at Philip. He did not react. "I love you." she said.

Anna pulled the trigger. The gun fired, and at the pop, there was nothing. Her body relaxed, but both Philip and the woman had disappeared. Anna was alone in the room. She slowly stood up from the bed, relaxing the gun at her side. Anna looked to where Philip and the figure were crouched, trying to calculate what had happened. She couldn't relate any reasoning to anything. They were gone. Nothing was left that said they had even been there in the first place. Even Anna's memory of the incident was fragmented. She backed out of the room, ready for anything that might jump out and surprise her. The house was silent, and she finally turned and headed for the door. No plan of where to go or what to do.

She only knew that she couldn't hang around here anymore. She walked up to the front door, and swung it open. Before she could step out, a familiar voice called out from behind her.

"Anna?"

She turned and saw Philip standing at the other end of the hall. She recognized him clearly now. Philip stood with his hands held out, one hand at his shoulder, the other slowly reaching for her. "Come on, honey. Just put the gun down."

"Philip?" Anna questioned.

Anna stood frozen, her back to the front door, holding the gun with both hands at her waist. Strange enough, even with her thoughts and intentions, having become almost instantly clear. She knew exactly where she was and who she was; the fog had lifted, but with clarity, came disorder. She had shot this man, her husband as it were, an act she didn't understand only a few moments ago, and one she comprehended even less now. How was he standing here, unharmed, and unaware of her actions? Or was he?

"Honey, please." Philip tried to talk her down calmly. He was genuinely lost as to his wife's actions, afraid not only for her safety but also his. "Why don't you tell me what's going on? Let me help you."

"You..." Anna started, "This isn't right." Anna was drowning in her disorientation. She stared through the floor, unable now to look at Philip. Although she remembered him, he appeared as someone that shouldn't be. He was a stranger, a person for all intent and purposes that was dead. She had shot him dead.

He is dead... Anna's mind began to stir again, this time with an even more disturbing notion. *He is dead!*

"Anna?" Philip tried again.

"None of this is real," Anna spoke in a hushed tone.

"What?"

"Something's wrong..." she continued, looking up at him, "You're dead."

Philip looked just as confused as his wife now, "Anna, I'm right here, hon." He took a slow step forward.

Anna snapped back in terror, raising the gun up at Philip, her trembling finger held dangerously on the trigger. Her whole body was shaking with fear. Something did not feel right for her, as if she had suddenly awoken in somebody else's body on a foreign planet.

Philip stiffened.

"Please, Anna," Philip tried again, slowly walking toward his wife, "Just put the gun..."

Anna fired!

Philip ricocheted against the wall and fell onto his side with a muffled thud. Anna stared down at his lifeless body. Anna dropped her arm to her side, her limbs beginning to lose their rigidity, slowly becoming like noodles. She leaned heavily against the door jamb to the kitchen, barely able to keep herself upright. While she continued to look onto her husband's, or what she could only perceive to be her husband's body, the sounds of tires skidding on asphalt and doors slamming shut weren't enough to draw her attention away.

"Ma'am!" A voice called out from behind her outside. "Police, ma'am! I need you to drop the gun!"

It didn't register with Anna at all, still paralyzed from the shock of the incident.

"Put the gun on the floor and put your hands in the air!" the voice called out again, this time more demanding.

Anna still hadn't moved, not realizing the officer had begun to enter the house behind her. "I need you to drop the gun, miss," The officer said firmly.

Finally, it registered what needed to be done. Anna let the gun fall from her fingers, still staring at the lifeless man beside her. The officers were quick to detain her, bringing her to the ground and cuffing her. On her chest, Anna was now inches from Philip's body. Not until the second officer had stepped in front of her, blocking her view, did Anna begin to cry. Uncontrollably, so, as they lifted her to her feet.

"Mrs. Doyer, you're under arrest." The officer could see that Anna was shaken, unable to keep her balance despite them holding her. "Mrs. Doyer, are you aware of your involvement in numerous hit and runs out on highway 28?"

Anna continued to break down, her breath becoming choppy with her mouth agape. She stumbled and lost her balance as the officers took her away. "This isn't real!" She screamed, "This isn't real! He isn't real! NO!" Anna struggled against the officer's weight. "You're not real. You can't be real!!!"

***

The room was blackened, with only the sharp twinkle of the control board lights blinking rapidly. A high-pitched alarm was wining as the lock snapped, and an attendant entered with Dr. Greenwood. They hurried to the control board, and Dr. Greenwood waited while his assistant typed in some quick commands.

"What's the problem?" Dr. Greenwood urged calmly.

"I don't know. The system's not responding."

Dr. Greenwood paced around the room, observing every crevasse he could. Perhaps there was something obvious out of place, a stray wire, a fuse, or God help him, a misconnection with the electrodes and the brain! But there was nothing he could see. Finally, he approached the podium as his assistant continued, "All the readouts are flat lined. Electrical activity is non-responsive. I'm showing no brain activity at all."

Dr. Greenwood typed in a simple command and looked up to the monitor. A few hum bars ignited. There was a soft pulse of light as the screen warmed up. A moment later, there was only one reading on the screen:

-NO SIGNAL-

Dr. Greenwood let out an exasperated sigh, hanging his head as he supported his weight on the podium. He then looked up, "What about the wife?"

His assistant typed a quick command. "She's still active," he said, looking to the doctor.

Dr. Greenwood collected his thoughts and stepped down, "Okay. We'll keep her program running." His tone was dull and unenthusiastic, a remarkable feet still, despite the setback. The disappointment was present in his gate, too, as he walked toward the exit. "I want to check and recheck everyone else in the network, see if there are any other anomalies." He paused. "I want round the clock observations, reports every hour. See if we can find out what happened."

Cole stepped closer to Dr. Greenwood, disappointed himself, but unsure how to empathize with the doctor, his friend. "Where do we go from here?"

Dr. Greenwood answered, more so to himself, "This is all they'll need to shut us down. There won't be any question." Cole waited still. Dr. Greenwood inhaled sharply, and headed toward the door, "Keep the active programs running. No new clients, though. I have to make some calls."

"Hey," Cole said as they exited, "this was an important first step. You made this a reality."

"Not sure how real it was," Dr. Greenwood said, looking around Cole's profile, unable to face his failure yet. He turned and departed as Cole pulled the door closed. The lock snapped back into place and plunged the room into darkness again. Indeed, it was a reality, one that only a few would ever know of.

For Anna, it would be one that she would never escape...

COLLATERAL

9:20pm

Stu might have felt nervous enough before, but once the bags had gone over their heads, it was no longer a situation he could ignore. He had to choke down a slight chuckle, thinking these kinds of things only happened in the movies, but this was obviously not the case here.

Along the way, Stu had lost track of how long the drive had been, only brave enough to ask of their situation once before. It was quickly discouraged, not physically, but verbally violent and forceful. He wasn't expecting to see him, much less find himself bound and blindfolded in a van on his way to God knows where. Despite this, perhaps on a reflex, he immediately called out, "Aaron?" This time, he was shoved into the side of the van. He didn't want to press the matter further; sooner or later, he would get his answers.

8:46pm

This was more than what he could say a few minutes ago when his friend—well, "friend"—first barged into the bar. Stu went into the Brookmill Tavern earlier for a quick drink, maybe two depending on his mood. Retrospectively, one should have been it, because as the second round of scotch was on its way, Stu's eye caught a commotion outside amongst the smokers. He couldn't see what or who it was but watched and waited to find out.

A figure moved through the crowd without regard for anyone else standing in his way. The people moved aside and exclaimed as the man walked to the door. Some of the more brazen smokers stood to obstruct, making the last few steps as difficult as possible. The man could see his effect on the people and calmed his approach, as not to incite any unwanted confrontations. He pushed cautiously inside.

Stu recognized the man immediately—Aaron; figuring that he was up to his usual antics. Aaron was nothing short of trouble; not enough where he couldn't keep himself on track, but just about anyone he encountered or reached out to for help, usually suffered from some ripple of his nonsense. Stu was wise to all this, and wanted nothing to do with Aaron tonight, but there was nowhere he could hide, or even sneak away to. It was a small room that always held an amazing number of patrons even on their busiest nights, except tonight. There were only a handful of people scattered about, but none so much that Stu could lose himself. He was stuck. He didn't have to look to notice the enthusiasm in Aaron's stride.

As casual as he tried to voice, "Hey! What's going on, man?" it was not successful. Aaron leaned against the bar stiff as aboard with a forced, but relieved smile on his face, standing elbow to elbow to Stu.

Stu could tell something was wrong, and worse, that Aaron would inevitably request assistance on some level. Any relief would do at this point, and it came in the form of, albeit briefly, the bartender, who came up with Stu's second round and asked Aaron if he wanted anything. Aaron stammered, fumbling through his pockets; Stu knew he didn't have any money and vouched for him. "Put it on mine."

Aaron smiled and ordered a beer. He relaxed once more, but Stu was counting the minutes in his head until the question came.

***

<u>9:32pm</u>

Christ! Another series of bumps! Whoever was driving didn't seem to have any regard for Stu's, or anyone's condition. *Why should they,* Stu wondered. These didn't seem like the kind of guys to concern themselves with legal matters, never mind and sense of decorum. Try as he might, Stu was unable to get any sort of answers from his captors.

Stu couldn't help but file through all the chances he had to end his encounter, and thus not have been where he was right now! As the drive progressed, it was easy to discern the change in terrain. The smooth hum of the asphalt had given way to the crumbling sounds of loose gravel and dirt under the moving car's weight. It swayed unevenly, dipping into the various divots and potholes. The car was taking frequent turns now, veering around corner after corner until coming to a stop.

They sat for a moment as if waiting for something. And, sure enough, they were. The van door slid open; hands came in and reached for Aaron first, then Stu, pulling him into the darkness.

8:55pm

It was as Stu had come to expect, enduring Aaron's effort of casual chitchat. They watched the games on TV, commenting here and there, and for a split second, Stu almost forgot what was coming. He didn't encourage it, but his posture shifted, and Stu braced himself on the bar, once again expectant.

"So, how's everything else going?" Aaron asked.

Here it comes…

Stu hesitated, debating whether to drag this out, or just get to it. "You don't need to do that," he said.

"What?"

"Just…" Stu waved him in, "tell me what's up?"

Aaron looked visibly relieved from his friend's invitation, and with it came a more genuine wave of anxiety. Aaron recited all of his prominent financial debts, many of which Stu was familiar with. Typical stuff like rent, bills, but one thing he didn't know about was Aaron's success in losing a significant chunk of change at the casino. Stu was not overly surprised until he found out it was more than three-thousand dollars! Suddenly, the stress on Aaron's face made more sense.

It was an issue that Aaron felt he could resolve with a simple loan, but no reputable company was going to lend him any money in his financial condition. He went on to explain that a friend had referred him to a place that would guarantee a payout to anyone. Desperate men do desperate things; this couldn't be a truer statement here.

Stu wondered how he could still be surprised after all these years but was simultaneously relieved. If it was money Aaron wanted, he could easily deny his help, since he didn't have the kind of cash Aaron may be looking to borrow.

"I know I fucked up, man," Aaron confessed, looking away from Stu.

"Yeah, that you did," Stu said with almost no sympathy. "And, I know you're in a pinch, but I can't help you."

Oddly, when Stu looked to Aaron to further his point, he got a strange sense from his friend. Though Aaron's expression was of disappointment, it came with a measure of fear. He also noticed that Aaron actively tried to avoid any eye contact as if there was something he didn't want to say. Stu's wish may have been granted if Aaron was to be giving up so easily. After all this time, he finally got the point that not everyone could save you. Stu went back to his scotch.

The front door swung open and in walked a tall suited man. He stood at the doorway, obstructing anyone's entrance or exit until he could survey the entire room.

Aaron's head snapped up at the creak of the door opening. Stu followed, observing slowly, less anxious. The uneasiness of the man's presence didn't settle, until they locked eyes. Stu's first impression was that of an undertaker come looking for a body that got away.

***

9:34pm

Still blindfolded, Stu didn't want to upset these guys anymore. It was a short walk he was reluctant to take, and quite difficult, as he dragged his feet along the rocks. Tripping over himself several times, he tried to hamper their efforts. It wasn't long before he could hear the stiff echo of their steps closing in to an approaching building. Wherever they were, it had to be out of the way; he heard no distant cars or any kind of ambient sound. No further words were exchanged, not with Stu or between the men. Stu tried to guess how many of them there were, but it was near impossible to say, save for the two strong grips that had his arms.

They walked through the threshold, their steps echoing down a long corridor. As they progressed, the tamping sounds of their shoes splashed apart shallow puddles, and the fine dirt crunched under their weight, making everything all the tenser. For some reason, Stu felt his movements were descending into hell or at the very least deep into the earth.

The walk went on, and on, forever straight until taking a sharp turn through another doorway. However far it was,

Stu eventually found himself in a cold, hollow room; the surrounding concrete was palpable, which played havoc on Stu's claustrophobia as he was sat in a waiting chair. His head snapped around, frantically trying to see through the blindfold. It didn't work.

"Wha—what is this?" Stu stammered, hyperventilating, "Where is this?!"

There was no answer. The men seemed to leave, pulling a heavy sounding metal door closed behind them. The bolt snapped into place, and Stu was now left alone, his heart thumping in his ear. His breath was sharp and short as he continued to try to see, but there was something more. His breath sounds became a means to read the room, a kind of sonar he tried to use. It sounded empty; only the chair in the apparent center, and...

"Is someone there?"

9:03pm

Aaron shifted in his spot. It was one of his many tells he gave away when trying to remain calm, though his posture turned to stone when the man approached. Stu looked back and forth from his friend and the suited man, curious. "You wanna tell me what's up?" Aaron didn't have time to answer.

The suited man came to a stop behind Aaron and Stu, not yet glancing at either of them. His eyes remained up, looking at the TV until the bartender approached.

"What can I get you, hon?" she asked.

It was a tense few seconds; even the bartender seemed uneasy waiting on the man's order. He kept staring up at the screen until finally, lowering his eyes to Stu's drink. "I'll have what he's having."

Stu turned to get a better look at him, only long enough to examine his appearance. He seemed neat and clean, very professional looking. A black on black suit that, further cementing the idea that this guy was an undertaker. He might even have passed for a Man in Black if given a black fedora. *There were no aliens here, not unless he were to count himself*, Stu thought, turning back around and trying to tend to his own business.

The bartender returned with his drink, another scotch on the rocks, setting it down between Aaron and Stu. She waited a moment for his money, while she casually observed the three men. Stu was clueless, and Aaron was tense, and she didn't want to know anything more, taking the man's money and running off to make change. She returned promptly to which the man gestured for her to keep it. Gratefully accepted, she nodded and kept to the far end of the bar.

The suited man reached between the two for his glass; only Stu watched him tip it back. Aaron kept his head down.

"How are you holding up, Aaron?" the man said calmly, his eyes still fixed above.

Aaron hesitated to answer, looking to Stu for some kind of prompt. "Okay." It was all he could muster.

"I'm sure." The man sipped his drink again. "So, is this your friend?"

Stu came to attention as he snapped his head around at the mention of his presence. His eyes darted between the suited man and Aaron. *Me?* Stu couldn't decide what to focus on first, the fact that the man was in some way here looking for him as well, or what it was Aaron had told him, or why he was even part of the conversation in the first place. Perhaps that was a good place to start...

"What? Me?" Stu began, "What about me?"

"As I understand it, your friend, here, has listed you as a reference in the outstanding debt he has amassed." Stu turned a slow, grim look to Aaron as the suited man continued. "This, unfortunately, makes you equally responsible for the ten-thousand dollars owed to my associates."

Stu's eyes burst open, staring a hole through Aaron. "What the hell is ten-thousand dollars?!" Stu hissed. "You just got done telling me it was three. Not that that's any better!"

***

<u>9:41pm</u>

Ten-thousand dollars! Stu couldn't even begin to imagine what Aaron would have needed that kind of money for, or why he would have sought out such shady people.

This wasn't any ordinary bank, obviously, but Stu didn't get the vibe that this was something of the mob either. But what did Stu know of the mob, outside of the movies, that is really?

It had been several minutes since he was secured to the chair, his arms and ankles bound to the cold metal bars. He could move if he so desired, but only in such a way to fall to the floor on his side, and then he'd go nowhere. Stu tried to maneuver about, scraping the metal feet of the chair along the concrete, producing a loud piercing screech that stabbed at his eardrums. Stu hissed, and heard another voice wince in pain as well.

"Hey!" Stu called out. He waited a few seconds for an answer, or to hear anything more. "Okay, I know someone's there! Come on!"

There was the mild sound of soft breathing, and then some dim approaching footsteps. He listened closely as the lock to the room was unbolted, and the door creaked open. "Hello?" Stu tried again.

A voice responded quietly, not to Stu, but another in there with them, "it's okay. Go wait outside."

Steps departed, and the door closed again; no lock this time.

'Mr. Arnought," A bold, imposing voice spoke.

"Who are you?" Stu asked back; his nerves were beginning to fray again.

"Mr. Arnought, we, um, we have a serious matter that needs resolving," the man spoke matter-of-factly.

"Look, whatever Aaron said to you... I have no idea what this is about, or who you are." Stu began as calmly as he could, his head snapping from side to side as if trying to see anything, "And, I'm plenty happy to stay blindfolded if you just want to drop me off in an ally somewhere. I won't ask questions, I—I won't..."

"Mr. Arnought, your friend has amassed a great debt with us, and has named you his... well, cosigner, if you will," the man said.

"I haven't signed anything!" Stu cried out.

It was nothing more than an impending formless voice to Stu, no footsteps could be heard, not even any kind of breathing from the speaking man, or anyone else with him, if there was anyone. *What was Aaron doing naming him for anything,* Stu wondered.

Stu tried to engage again, "What did he need the money for?"

"We don't know, and we don't ask," the voice said plainly. "It's none of our concern. This is, though."

"Is Aaron here?" Stu asked. "Can I talk to him? Find out what this is all about?"

Denied. Once again, less is more. The man wasn't concerned with any outside conditions, only the matter at hand, which was that of a ten-thousand-dollar debt owed.

Money's green no matter who pays, and, well, regardless of who posts the collateral, it was all in equal value.

"I don't know why he named me," Stu began, "but I don't have that kind of money. This is the first I'm hearing about it. Please!"

The man let out a long, disappointed sigh, almost as if he was upset about what had to be done. "Okay," he said in a flat tone. Stu heard the dirt crunching under their shoes as they rotated on the balls of their feet, turning to leave. He could make out at least three discernible sets of footfalls walking out of the room before the door was pulled closed again, and the lock snapped back into place. This time he couldn't hear anyone else in the room with him, only his lonely shuddering breathing echoing off the cold concrete walls.

"The Fu—" Stu tried to brush the blindfold on his shoulder to lift it off his eye, but it was no use. He relaxed to think, to take a breath, listening to the footfalls departing down the corridor. They came to a stop. The sound of another lock being opened shot down the hall. That was all; Stu could not hear anything now. If they were in another room, it had to be where they were keeping Aaron.

9:12pm

Fuck me, ten-thousand dollars!

Aaron tried like hell to rope Stu into the conversation, but so long as the suited man didn't address him directly, Stu made efforts to stay out of it.

"We can discuss this further outside, Aaron," the suited man stated, extending his hand to the door.

Aaron stood fast against the bar, stiffened in fear, which Stu noticed. Normally, Stu wasn't shy about going to bat for a friend, but seeing as Aaron might have involved Stu in some of his typical mischief, Stu wanted no part of it. It hurt to do so. He wouldn't look Aaron in the eye until he stood up to leave.

The suited man waited patiently for Aaron to gather himself together; clearly, Aaron had no other option, anything he could do to avoid the confrontation. Aaron stepped away from the bar and was guided out.

Stu finally turned to watch his friend walk outside. Stu noticed that no one around seemed to pay either of them any sort of attention, as if they weren't even there.

"You having another one, honey?" the bartender asked, calling Stu's attention back.

"No, thank you."

Stu sat quietly, keeping to himself with his eyes once again fixed on the TV above. It didn't take long for the weight of the situation to bare down on him, and the thought of what might be happening to his friend began to bother. He didn't want to be any more involved than he apparently was, but he couldn't sit by and let Aaron suffer, as much as he wanted to let tough-love teach him a lesson. Stu finished up his drink and got up to leave, forgetting to leave a tip.

Stepping outside, Stu looked around for either of them, but they were nowhere in sight. The last remaining smokers were just finishing up, pinching their cigarettes in the steeple which bellowed out a rancid grey curl of smoke. Stu ventured toward the parking lot, away from the warm lighting and into the empty void of night. The parking lot was absent of any sort of life, at least that Stu could see. As long as he's been coming here, there have never been any lamplights for the parking lot. His own intension was clear, that if he couldn't find Aaron, he would move on his way and try to call him tomorrow.

Stu paused at the car door, taking one last look around. His eyes had yet to adjust to the darkness, seeing only the street lights from the bar shone on the road. It was a silent moment that felt too quiet for comfort, and Stu fumbled for his keys despite no one around to see him. He tried to maintain his calm persona, attentively masking his nervousness for his ego. Before he could open the door, a bag was abruptly pulled over his head and cinched tightly around his neck. It was swift and silent, with such precision that whoever it was, no doubt the suited man from a moment ago was able to clamp a hand over Stu's mouth to keep him from alerting anyone in ear shot. Stu was dragged along a few feet into a waiting van only a few spaces away. *How could I have not seen something so close,* he wondered.

***

9:52pm

AAHHHHHH! AHH-AAHHHHHH!

It was Aaron screaming; the sounds were nothing but unintelligible belts of pain that ripped down the hollow corridor. It only lasted a few moments until he fell silent, which somehow was more unsettling that his cries. At least then, Stu knew he was alive; he wasn't so sure now. His breathing quickened and became stiff and sharp.

"Oh, fuck... fuck..." Stu panicked.

Stu tried to free himself again, more desperately this time, with the motivation of uncertain torture helping him ignore the pains in his wrist and ankles. Small in comparison to what might be coming, he figured. He could feel the cuts forming under the ties and the wet sensation of his blood beginning to run, but still, he twisted and rotated his limbs, hoping for some lose end. But if he were loose, where would he go? It didn't matter at this point, if only to give himself a fighting chance, he'd take that over being tortured any time.

Stu winced in pain, and then paused to catch his breath. He could hear the indistinct chatter from down the hall, most likely from the men who had just "collected" what they were after from Aaron. Stu felt for his friend, but wasn't ready to endure this!

The voices continued for a minute before going quiet, followed by the gentle tapping of their approaching footfalls. Stu panicked as they grew closer; his breath froze again in his chest as he could hear the lock being tinkered with again, the bolt being snapped open.

The door creaked open, and he could hear the men enter and surround him on both sides and another stepping closer.

"So, unfortunately, your friend was unable to account for the money he was due," the man said in a monotone.

"Look, "Stu started, "I don't know—who you are, okay? I don't know what any of this is, or where..." His sentences became fragmented as his nerves fired up, seizing his entire body. "But I can't do anything for him. I can't—I don't know why he borrowed the money. I knew nothing about it until tonight. I..." Stu was beginning to lose track of his words. His head remained stiff and focused as if he could see through the blindfold.

"Mr. Arnoguht, it makes no difference to us where the money comes from, just as long as we are paid what we are owed on time," the man stated. "Now, we are mere employees of some considerably powerful people, you understand, and our job is simple. Collect our money, or the insurance."

The word 'insurance' sent a tinge up Stu's spine. What did they want?

"What..? Insurance? What do you mean?"

"It's a simple matter of ten-thousand dollars, Mr. Arnoguht. How do you plan on acquiring our money?" the man asked.

"I…" Stu tried to look around, hoping for a glimpse of some faces to go with the disembodied voice that was speaking to him. "I don't have that kind of money!" Stu admitted. "I live in a shitty apartment, and I was just laid off, I…"

There was a pause. "Okay, then" The man stated as if he were accepting the simple facts of a deal.

The footsteps scuffed the floor rapidly as the men moved around. There were no more words, just movements all around him, and the light banging sounds of some metal items being tampered with. Amidst it all, Stu heard the striking of a flint followed by the pop of a butane torch being lit. "What's this!?" Stu screamed, jerking up and down in the chair. Oddly, it gave the men the opportunity they were looking for, as two of them had taken hold of Stu's pants and pulled them down to his ankles. The sudden shock of his bare ass hitting the cold metal chair kept him off balance and unnerved even more now!

"What are you doing!?" he yelled repeatedly.

"You got him?" another voice asked as an arm come around his waist, holding him firmly to the chair.

Stu continued to struggle against their onslaught until he could feel hands maneuvering around his genitals. His brain didn't know how to distinguish what was happening right now. Violated, tortured, Stu didn't know what was happening, at least until he felt the knife's cold edge under his groin. The thought came to him, but he was unable to process it in time before he felt the blade cutting into his flesh. The pain was excruciating as Stu screamed until he could feel a burning sensation in his throat, burning his vocal cords. The fact that he could feel anything more on top of what was happening was a miracle itself.

It was relatively quick, with only a few long slices before it was done. Stu could feel the blood rushing to his head, as well as the rapidly growing pool under his seat. "Hurry up," one of the men said before Stu felt another wave of agony. It was to cauterize the wound, a searing iron rod was held to his now vacant crotch. Stu's exhausted screams came in waves as the smell of burning flesh filled the room.

All this thrashing about, Stu's blindfold had fallen off of one eye, and for the first time, he was able to see through his tear-filled wandering eye the calm, collected faces of the men, each wearing similar dress suits as was the man at the bar, though he was not present. Their job seemed done as they were now gathering up their things and hauling them out of the room.

"We'll be back to take him out in a minute," one of them said as they left.

Stu's body fell limp, even as hard as he tried to remain conscious, bobbing his head as if his neck were made of a loose rope. His vision started to fade in and out, but for a brief moment, what became the last image he could remember was the grim sight of his severed penis lying on the floor in front of him in a pool of blood. The sight radiated through his body, to which he finally passed out.

However long it was, Stu eventually came to in the parking lot at the bar, apparently left next to his car. Nothing was missing... well, nothing he couldn't live without.

A MURDER

No coverage, not even one bar, the battery was near dead anyway. No way for Karl to find out what was taking his brother so long; he sat nervously in the car, waiting. It was still daytime, but there was an overcast, and the sky had a perfectly even dullness, so there was no way to tell what time of day it was, much less which direction was north or south or anything else for that matter. A two-lane blacktop road snaked up into the distance and disappeared into some trees, or a forest if you wanted to get technical about it. It also snaked down toward some lumpy hills and disappeared there as well. In the distance, the furious sound of a two-stroke chainsaw ripped through the air. This had been happening more often lately, but it was impossible to tell whether it was up in the forest or down in the lumpy hills. Two different ways to go, with a dead battery and no bars, and nobody left to blame.

It didn't matter which way they went, Karl only wanted to be anywhere else now, far away from here. He was a younger man in his early twenties, with a quiet sort of innocents about him, although innocent was the last word he would use to describe himself today or any day here after. Karl sat in their father's late-model Cadillac El Dorado with his back straight, his head tilted back and his eyes closed, praying desperately, silently, holding back every emotion he had.

Silence was something Karl was becoming accustomed to. His progressive hearing loss was so that he was almost completely dependent on a hearing aid, which he now cradled in his hand on his lap. Without it, sounds—the ones that he could register—came through muffled and pulsing as if he were listening to the world through a wall. He was able to distinguish enough to get by, but Karl wanted silence now, and for the most part, he got it.

He kept his eyes closed, trying his best to ignore the chainsaw's reoccurring noise that seemed to vibrate in his head. He wasn't certain before, but after hearing it on and off since Donnie left—*God, where was he*—he knew there was someone nearby quartering a thick tree trunk. Wherever it was coming from, they were too close, and Karl became increasingly nervous.

It's amazing, he thought; *a chainsaw—I'm sure of it.* He could recall familiar sounds simply by their vibrations that hummed dully in his ear. Hell, he could sometimes read the mood of a room by the tone alone, not needing to hear what was being said. But all he could hear now was Kimberly's screams echoing in his head.

For one night of erotic pain that ended almost twenty-four hours ago, he wished, through the grief and humiliation of his own psyche, that he had listened more closely to Kimberly's cries of pain. His hands around her neck made that impossible, though it was her that placed them there, he couldn't distinguish the urgency of the situation. Had he known, he might not have killed her. Sex was awkward enough for him, and his girlfriend's imagination had definitely tested his confidence. He accepted this ceaseless recurring of last night as punishment. If only it would end here; he knew it wouldn't, though. Karl remained quiet, impatiently waiting, as he brought his hands up in clenched fists to his forehead trying to hold back the tears.

Karl still couldn't explain what happened to his brother, Donnie. They were as close as any siblings could get, and Donnie had become somewhat of a caretaker for him, but nothing could have prepared him for what he saw last night. After Karl had explained what they were doing, Donnie's expression was the first real confirmation of this twisted happening. He watched Donnie's face contort with every detail wondering what happened that could've escalated so far. Karl had been incoherent since the incident, and was mostly catatonic for the duration of the ride, and despite his brother's efforts, Karl couldn't communicate, or maybe he didn't want to.

Karl's patience began to fray, wondering what was taking Donnie so long; (not that Karl knew any specifics of hiding a body in the woods) it had been almost two hours. *Shouldn't he have been back by now?* A semi-truck roared by, rocking the car from side to side and shaking Karl from his slumber. A rush of nervous energy surged through his body, and he snapped his head back, looking up and down the road; only the departing trailer of the truck in the distance, nothing more. However, something he could not explain but an unmistakable sensation, he could feel the stare of many eyes watching him, small penetrating and guilty eyes peering right through him. Outside, the trees were busy with numerous crows, swooping from branch to branch. It made Karl mad thinking that they were looking at him; that they knew what had happened—what was happening. *Come on, Donnie!* Karl buried his face in his hands a moment before a figure began to emerge from the woods.

Grimy, filthy with dirt and sweat, his brother finally appeared, taking heaving strides up the embankment and out of the darkened forest. He came to rest at the guardrail, leaning against the cold metal with his head hung low between his arms; sweat glistened off his brow. Donnie looked like he may keel over at any minute. He took in a few deep breaths to compose himself before looking up to his brother, grateful that Karl was still there. Not that he had anywhere to go, but after last night, Donnie didn't know what to expect anymore. He certainly never expected he would be using his car, a gift from their father's will, as a hearse. Donnie wiped a bead of sweat from his eyebrow and straightened up. Before he could climb the rail, he, too, was greeted by another of the malevolent birds. It came down from the trees and landed on the rail beside him. Its claws tapped lightly as the bird continued to adjust its stance, not threatened at all by Donnie's presence. It rattled out a casual throaty caw, staring at him with penetrating curiosity. The crow flapped one wing, then the other, and was mildly startled by a passing car. Similarly startled, Donnie hesitated, stepping over the rail. *Had I been seen?* He started to craft a lie in his head, just in case. *I was only taking a leak*. He crouched slightly out of view waiting for the car to pass, holding his breath as if somehow it would have helped him, as the soft rushing sound of the car cutting through the wind drove by. A cool breeze trailed behind, and Donnie stepped over. At the same time, the crow had managed to hop back on the rail.

Donnie approached the car, watching for any more potential witnesses that might drive by as he came around to the back of the car to the open trunk. It was quiet again except for the soft sound of the leaves wisping in the sky, and the ever-distant hissing and ticking noises of grasshoppers and locust all about the woods. It was tranquility, at least that's what it was meant to be, but Donnie's heart skipped a beat as he looked into the dark abyss of the wilderness where the secret, he hoped, would remain. As he put a hand on the trunk lid, the distant droning hum of the chainsaw came to life once again and began to go to work on another tree limb. Donnie perked up, looking toward the sound, and yet another potential prying eye. They had to leave—now!

The trunk slammed shut, snapping Karl out of his own thoughts. He spun around in time to see Donnie open the door. Karl turned, and Donnie slumped in the seat, not sharing a look with Karl before pulling his door closed. The shame had once again taken hold, and Karl hung his head, trying to hold back the tears.

Did all of that really just happen? Donnie could barely bring himself to look at Karl as he aggressively massaged his forehead in an effort, he vainly hoped, to press hard enough and erase the events of the last twenty-four hours. He took a deep breath, exhaled long, and then put a comforting hand on his brother's shoulder. *We'll figure this out*. Karl finally allowed himself to cry.

All their life they had been inseparable even with Karl's condition looming, and worsening over time. In some ways, his condition made things between them even more personal. He would do anything for his brother (obviously), and he knew Karl felt the same, but Donnie couldn't make peace with what he wanted to do here and what he knew had to be done. In fact, Donnie had buried a body in the woods for Karl, and he was questioning himself on what to do next. It was written all over his face.

Donnie needed to breathe, and Karl needed to rest, and he knew that sooner or later, their mother would be wondering where they were.

Donnie checked his phone, this being the third time since they arrived, and still, there was nothing. Was he really expecting something different? He put his phone in the console and turned the power on, leaving the engine off. The dashboard –PINGED—an alert with the gas icon lighting up. *More good news*, Donnie thought. How long had they been driving; since last night… all day!? And worse, Donnie looked around and wondered if he knew where they were

Donnie continued to ponder the situation with the details of the dark reality beginning to crash down around them, a bird—another crow landed hard on the hood, its bony claws tapping a rhythmic beat on the metal resonated in the cab. Donnie and Karl gasped and shot back against the bench seat until they realized what it was. They watched, as the bird walked about the hood, inspecting them with its own cold suspicion. They remained still until it let out a single caw and flew away into the trees.

It was time to go. *Where to*, Donnie wondered. He didn't know how much farther they could go, or how to get back home. If only they weren't in such a precarious position, they could ask someone for help. But someone was close by, as the chainsaw reverberated through the trees once again. The sound made Karl perk up while at the same time, Donnie turned to him with a slight sense of levity. He touched his ear, to which Karl nodded. Donnie looked out the window, it was as good a chance as any, then started the car and pulled onto the road.

Apart from the few cars and trucks that had passed by earlier, they seemed to be the only ones on the road. The sky was still a flat grey and darkening. Though it didn't feel like rain, the air was cooling, and Donnie knew it was getting late. About a mile up the road, they came to a clearing, a dirt road—a driveway—that ran a narrow path into the woods. At the driveway's mouth was an oversized, black mailbox with the name Miller and the address number one-thousand and three. Nailed to a tree above was an aged sign with faded lettering which read: -Private Property-. Not something they wanted to cross as they pulled off the road onto the driveway. Karl beckoned Donnie to keep on driving, telling him that they have to come across something sooner or later. But how far could they go? No gas, no phone, and where they were; these were all things that Donnie felt needed attention now. They were lost, but to be stranded as well would complicate matters further.

While they looked around the area for anything more in the way of direction (there was nothing at all) they noticed the crows busy in the trees. Dark patches that danced about and swooped to the ground, and from tree to tree, cawing and fussing with one and other. It seemed strange, ominous even. To focus on one meant you couldn't see the rest, but to look to the sky, the trees came to life. *A murder*, Donnie couldn't help but think, the breath being taken out of his lungs—*A murder of crows.*

Donnie took one more look at the gas needle, which was now obscuring the E. Taking a chance, he instructed Karl to put in his hearing aid. Their first priority had to see about getting some gas, and that finding the source of the noise was their best option. Karl's expression conveyed his objections, but there was nothing he could do. Donnie turned, and they headed down the driveway, into the wilderness yet again.

They were here, too, the crows, littering the trees all around. It began to feel as though there was something else around, something they could not see. Or maybe, Donnie thought, they were an omen of some kind, a reminder of the atrocity they had participated in, never to leave them in peace. Karl paid no attention to the activities above. His eyes were fixed out his window, staring into, and through the woods. They sat in silence once again; Donnie wanted to say something, but God only knew what was going on inside his brother's head.

The silence in the car was tense. It wasn't far before the path turned at an extreme angle, losing sight of where they had come. The only sound that broke through was the crumbling of the dirt and rocks under the weight of the car. Further and further in, Donnie grew more uneasy, shifting his weight around and consciously holding his gaze out his side of the car watching the woods run by. If their deed was found... it was a thought they both had, but didn't want to entertain. Perhaps, this was a subconscious intention of his, giving himself a nagging reminder (as if he needed one) to handle the situation when they were in a better position. As they continued, they passed by another sign:

-NO TRESPASSING- this one, less strategically placed but more as a reminder, one that they promptly ignored as a clearing began to emerge ahead.

It was nothing far from what they expected coming to a clearing which looked more like a scrap yard than a place of residence. There were rusted relics of cars half-buried in the ground, piles of forgotten tools and engine parts that were gathering outside a small storage shed. The home itself looked as though it was in a constant state of repair. It resided in a shadow of itself, and with the steady incline of the mountain side, rising up behind it gave the impression that this place was the start of a very deep and cavernous tunnel. A passage to Hell, perhaps, the way their day was going, why not? At the far corner of the house was the incomplete log resting on a pair of sawhorses next to an ever-expanding pile of quartered wood, with an orange chainsaw resting next to it; *explains that*. Among all this, Donnie prayed for a quick solution; directions, some gas would be ideal. He'd find his own way out if he could. They parked the car off to the side, as out of the way and as far away as he could.

Donnie put the car in park and took a quick look around. He told Karl to stay put while he got some help. Karl had no response, slumped back into his seat, turned his head, and looked back out the window. Donnie took his phone and exited the car with a heavy sigh, reluctant—

cautious might be more accurate—in every step he took forward.

Karl watched his brother approach the house. There was nothing to listen for, nothing he wanted to hear, and he took out his hearing aid once again.

Walking through the yard, the forgotten land as he thought of it, Donnie was able to get the full humbling scope of the area. Standing in the palm of the surrounding tall lush pines, Donnie was almost able to forget their situation, taking in the awe-inspiring sight. However, the dark reminder was present here, too; a single crow coasted in and perched itself on the corner of the house—the winged demon. Donnie cursed it silently in his head as he stepped onto the porch.

Karl became restless, readjusting himself from side to side, as if he were sitting on a pile of unforgiving rocks. He leaned over and pulled the latch for the trunk. When it popped open, he stepped out of the car with slight hesitation. He wasn't sure what it was he meant to look for, but his instinct drew him out.

Coming around the back, Karl paused before looking into the trunk. The faint feeling that Kimberly's body might still be in there sent a chill through him, and he closed his eyes before turning to see. It was empty, but the shroud of guilt was still very much present. Karl stared down into the cold hollow, resting a hand on the lid, and for the first time, he allowed himself to examine what had happened. How had the situation gotten so out of hand? He couldn't recall, perhaps mercifully so. The last memory he did have was of kneeling over Kimberly's lifeless body in tears, holding her hand tightly when Donnie had come in. They had talked, well Donnie had talked, and in a panic, maybe in an attempt to protect his brother, had encouraged him to move the body out. From there, it was one impulsive decision after another.

Donnie had not intended to drive out this far, had not meant to pick such a random location, and had no forethought of what to do next, but here they were. Karl had tried to figure out an answer, almost as hard as Donnie had found it to ask the question, but all he could say was that Kimberly made him do it. It became a response that neither of them wanted to explore further.

Karl looked up to where Donnie was still waiting on the porch, eclipsed in the shaded blind of the roof, righting himself up and relaxing his shoulders a bit. To his right, he saw movement, a young girl stepping out from behind the wood pile. She stood there staring at him for a moment, a slight curious smile tugging at the corner of her mouth. Karl was frozen. He couldn't help but see the resemblance; the same slender build, the same innocent looking features in her expression. The only differences were her clothes, old and worn—almost certainly second hand, and her hair. Hers was longer, darker, and draped over her shoulders, reaching down to her waist. Before Karl could think of what to do, the girl reached an arm out and made sudden strides toward him. The thought of this being Kimberly, in some grim fashion having come back for him, sent a wave of terror through his body. He stumbled backward, tripping over his foot. He landed with a thud that knocked the wind out of him as he slid across the dirt. A plume of dust surrounded him, blinding his view of the girl. He didn't see her again until she reached out and stroked his cheek.

She held her hand there for a moment; her expression fell to an impatient stare, replacing her dainty smile. Less afraid, now, but more curious, Karl looked up to see the darkness in her eyes. They were severely dilated, dark pits of black, as if nothing were there. He felt nervous about how she was looking at him, like some kind of prophet of impending doom. He may have remained cowered on the ground if Donnie hadn't come running over.

Along with him was a young man of about the same age as Donnie, gruff and trim, the weathering of the sun left him with a leathery skin showing he was a working man, possibly the one working with the saw all the while. He stood next to the girl, over Donnie, who knelt, working on hoisting Karl to his feet. More people—not exactly what Karl was expecting, or wanted. He stole another brief look at the girl. Kimberly's image still imprinted over her, and he turned to walk away, but Donnie held him firm.

Donnie tried to tell him that everything was alright, and found that Karl's responses weren't lining up with his own words. He looked in Karl's ear and saw that his hearing aid was out. Sighing, frustrated, but he understood that now wasn't the time to scold him about anything, and Donnie flashed his brother a quick, "It's OK" gesture.

Calming a bit, Karl turned a plastic but polite smile to the strangers. He gave a slight nod to the man with Donnie, who they later found out, was her brother, Eddie.

In the distance, an older woman approached, presumably their mother, a small, thin grey-haired woman homely dressed.

They continued to talk amongst themselves, but Karl could not gather the courage to look to the girl again, making a conscious effort not to. He could not bear another suggestion of Kimberly.

While Karl replaced his hearing aid at Donnie's request, he noticed the girl's eyes, sad and empathetic, were fixed on his device. Her name was Tabitha, and she was also deaf, but unlike Karl, her affliction was without any reprieve. She was mute, yet her eyes said plenty; stricken black and hollow, even more so now that Karl was able to see clearer. As disturbing as they were, Karl wondered if Donnie had noticed her, or either of the other two as Karl looked on them. They, too, had their eyes stricken in a deep vantablack. Was this anything at all to be concerned about? Karl had no time to contemplate this or share his concerns with his brother, as he was now being led toward the house. He felt his objections would've been radiating strong enough that Donnie might catch on, but he didn't. After what they had been through,

Karl wasn't willing to bring any unwarranted attention to himself, hoping he could be a simple figure in the background for however long they were going to be here.

The light was fading, the sky fell into a deeper ashy grey, and as they stepped up onto the porch, they fell under a consuming shadow. In that shroud, the strangers smiled at two crows skipping along the rails. Donnie had finally addressed their abundant presence, to which their mother, Grace, had simply said that they were part of the family. Continuing on, they stepped inside, the screen door creaked before snapping shut, and the crow gave an ingenuous caw.

Inside, the house was rustic décor with no nook of any shelf or wall left bare. It was a somewhat constricting but comforting environment. Under normal circumstances, this would have been an inviting atmosphere, but this was anything but normal.

Karl stood there awkwardly, unsure how to react or respond to anything as Donnie went back and forth with Grace, letting on vague lies about what they were doing out here. The only fact that was true about any of it was their issue of running out of gas. Worried Karl might give their deceit away, Donnie shot him a glance. Thankfully, he just appeared tired.

Karl kept his gaze, down looking through the rest of them, but never losing sight of Tabitha, who was again staring at him in a peculiar way. Karl's eye lids began to fall despite his efforts to keep them open. This they noticed, and

Grace offered to let Karl relax while Donnie went out with Eddie to get gas.

Donnie had his objections, suggesting that Karl come along. Because of his condition and the circumstances they were in—he was laying it on pretty thick—he felt it best for them to remain together, and not impose on their family any longer than they already have. Karl looked up and took a step toward the door, but Tabitha took his arm. Karl stopped and looked back, seeing the warm expression on her face. She wanted him to stay.

Grace insisted further while Eddie walked toward the front door and situated himself, putting on his coat and making sure he had his keys. Grace said he would be looked after and that she would have some food ready by the time they returned; if they had to leave, they would do so with full stomachs. Admittedly, they were very kind and accommodating, but no gesture could take their minds from their true business. *How long could they keep this façade up,* Donnie wondered.

They had learned to garner much between each other from a slight glace, as Donnie turned a look to Karl. He mentioned that it might be a good idea for Karl to lie down for a bit while he was gone. He could tell Karl was uncomfortable with this, but at the same time, he could barely keep his eyes open, his head repeatedly nodded off, forcing him to catch himself before falling asleep on his feet. He'd be crazy if he wasn't worried, but Donnie knew in their brief second of eye contact that Karl wouldn't say anything to trouble himself. He told Karl to rest, sleep if he could, and that he'd be back soon enough. Donnie requested if he could plug in his phone to charge while he was gone. Grace nodded pleasantly, and Donnie handed the phone to Karl.

He was uneasy but too exhausted to express as such, as Donnie departed. The door closed, and Karl turned to Tabitha, who still had a gentle grip on his arm. Grace told him that Tabitha would take him upstairs to get some rest, that for anything, he needed only to ask. She was very polite, too polite, one might even say, but Karl smiled.

Tabitha had released his arm for the banister as they climbed the stairs, with each one creaking and groaning in their own unique way. Some so intensely, it could be felt through their shoes. If one were so in tune with them, they could properly navigate their way in the pitch blackness. Walking up, Karl found himself disoriented; the stairwell appeared warped and askew, like something of a funhouse corridor. He half expected the figures in the dusty oil paintings to look his way (they did, but it was only the familiar illusion seen a hundred times over; good art followed you when you moved) as they passed. At the summit, they took a sharp U-turn by an undersized, somewhat ineffective railing that came up only to Karl's waist. Loose, too, as Karl put a hand on it to measure how low it was. It fit the rest of the house, with the narrow hallways and short paths from one room to another; it was a snug fit for anyone who lived here. Some might call it cozy or congested.

They came to a door at the end of the hall, about four steps from the stairs. The only light was a small brass lamp on an end table in the corner by the door that burned like candle light. Even with modern accommodations, it still felt like a house that was stuck in the 1800s. It was musty, damp, and cool, a definite place of meager standards. Tabitha opened the door and stepped in, Karl followed.

Karl stood there a moment until Tabitha guided him over and sat him down at the edge of the bed. In the warm, dimly lit room, she sat down next to him and held his hand. It was dark, but she could see the pain in his eyes, the emptiness, and loss he was feeling. Karl looked down at their hands, and for a brief moment, perhaps a means of coping with the situation, he felt that this was truly Kimberly holding his hand, or maybe he wanted it to be. *She's up there, alone he* thought; where would they be had nothing happened? Slowly, he brought his eyes up to hers and once again found himself looking at Kimberly's likeness. It became too much of an emotional wave for him, and Karl sat with his head in his hands, letting out an exhaustive breath. He heard a soft flapping by the window and didn't look up until he heard the bird come inside.

Another crow had hopped from the window sill and was walking across the floor, toward Tabitha. She turned and smiled, and moved out of the way, as the bird jumped onto a nearby wooden laundry rack. It rattled as the crow settled in, standing there as if it were now waiting for something. Karl thought no further, as Tabitha returned, and put a hand on his shoulder, guiding him back to lie down, helping him settle in. Karl felt a little awkward, unable to get comfortable as his head hit the pillow. Tabitha sat next to him, gently stroking his forehead until he closed his eyes. The ordeal had finally weighed him down enough, and Karl fell asleep.

Karl awoke, startled, spinning to his back and propping himself up onto his elbows. How long had it been, hours? He couldn't remember where he was or why he was here. But the grace of ignorance expired when he saw Tabitha standing over him. She had a familiar smile. Karl rotated to the edge of the bed and sat, once again unable to look at Tabitha, who stood patiently, waiting, holding a glass of pale yellow liquid. He stood and came to the window as everything began to come back to him, looking out for his brother wondering where he was, or how long he'd been gone. Something felt off; something had to be... *CAW*—the bird! He had forgotten it was there! It jumped back and spread its wings wide, ready to fight or fly at a moment's notice.

Karl didn't notice Tabitha had approached him. She placed a hand on his shoulder. He turned, finally able to look at her without hesitation. They stood close. His heart throbbed for a moment, feeling as though he could kiss her if the opportunity presented itself. As if listening to his thoughts, Tabitha put a hand to his chest—to his heart—and Karl brought his to her hand. She glanced over his shoulder to the unyielding crow and smiled. Still smiling, she found Karl's eyes again and set the glass in his hand. *What is this*, he asked with his eyes. Responding, she sipped the drink and handed it back to him. Hesitating, Karl touched the liquid to his tongue—it was a bitter taste that aerosolized on contact. Karl coughed at the sudden burst of clarity, indeed freeing his head of any congestion. It was some trouble to drink, but very refreshing and worth the effort. Country people always have interesting remedies for all manner of ailments, physical or mental. He sipped it continuously, until there was nothing more.

Tabitha smiled wide, as Karl took in a deep breath, the first real clean air he tasted since he could remember. A minute stir of disorientation had knocked him off balance for a moment, but it wasn't anything new for him today. While admiring her warm, attractive smile, Karl caught a glimpse of white light sweeping through the trees. He went to the window in time to see headlights wash over the yard and come to rest next to their car. Donnie was back, finally! He watched his brother and Eddie climb out of the car and attended to the El Dorado, presumably filling it with gas. Karl was relieved, they would be leaving soon! He turned to Tabitha with a smile, which slowly melted down his face until his mouth was agape. Tabitha tilted her head, curious, *what's wrong?*

Behind her, the crow rattled and clicked. To his horror, next to the crow, stood a man in the shadows, facing the wall; bald, with greyish skin, shivering and depleted looking. What little clothes he had on were torn and uneven, filthy and wet. He stood in the corner like that of a punished child. Karl stared at him, terrified and awestruck. Was this someone who had been standing there the whole time that he hadn't noticed? Karl took a cautious step forward, then another, extending his arm out in front of him. An inch from him now, his fingers should have touched him, but he felt nothing. His hand moved through the man's torso until it touched the wall; still nothing. The crow 'cawed' and 'rattled' again, and Karl pulled his hand back in a panic as if he were afraid he might lose it. He looked to the girl and saw that her eyes were again wide and black, dark holes of emptiness. He wondered if his were the same. The tea! It was the only thing he could think of! Tabitha looked back to where the man and the crow were, then to Karl. She looked perfectly calm, wondering why Karl was so shaken. Karl stumbled back as the realization came over him, nearly tripping over himself.

In the hall, he saw several more crows perched on the stunted rail by the stairs. Their 'caws' and 'clicks' stopped Karl in his tracks as he once again laid eyes on two more disembodied peoples standing by the stairs looking into nothingness, it seemed. One of them, he thought, looked familiar, but Karl wasn't at all interested in staying to find out. Making his way to the stairs and trying to avoid any contact with the *ghosts*, he couldn't help think of them as anything but; if they were like the one in the room, he wouldn't be able to touch them, and he didn't take his eyes off of their decomposing appearances.

Donnie entered with Eddie, in time to find Karl hurdling down the stairs, leaning on the banister and tripping over one step after another. He yelled at Karl to calm down, meeting him at the bottom and holding him still. Karl looked back up the stairs to where Tabitha stood (the discorporated souls milling around, seemingly unaware of her presence). One, a child of about twelve, looked to Karl and reached a decayed hand out for him. She smiled, and Karl was able to see the features of her face. Her eyes were hollow and black, and her skin was dried out and cracked, like that of a porcelain doll. She came down the stairs, glided, and Karl broke away from his brother, running for the door.

Out on the porch, Karl burst through the door, stumbling to his knees. His sudden presence scattered dozens of crows that 'cawed' and 'rattled' as Donnie came out to pull his brother up. Standing nearby, a legion of decaying apparitions ushered him along, among which Karl could see one that resembled his deceased father. But the rest were disembodied strangers, examining him with curiosity, and studying all of his secrets. He settled until one undeniable face stepped out of the crowd. Watching her, Karl fell back into his brother's arms, attempting to leap away and get back inside. It was Kimberly, as she was now without any life in her face. Karl could see the blood on her lip that ran from her nose, and the bruise around her neck, the one that he had inflicted her with, which led to her death. This is a punishment; the sentiment was conveyed with a single scream, as he watched her approach. Her blank stare held her sorrow, an image that would forever be imprinted into his mind. Donnie picked his brother up and headed back to their car, as the Miller family watched with stone faces.

The brothers made their way through the crowd and back to the El Dorado where a crow flew directly over their heads. It landed on the hood, looking at them. Another crow flew overhead and landed beside it. The first crow squawked, and then both birds flew away. The brothers looked to each other, and then got in the El Dorado. Only one way to go, now with five bars and a full battery.

PEN PAL

Dear Amy,

I feel like I can confide in you; I hope I'm not overstepping my grounds. You've been a good friend to me these last few months despite our never meeting face to face, although I hope to have the opportunity soon. I found this letter a difficult one to pen with us being only silent voices to one and other—where does the line get drawn in such a relationship?

First, let me start by saying what I have done was not without reason, although I'm sure my reasons won't be accepted by many—if any. I know I can count on you, though. I was given permission. Well, permission might not be the right word; they had told me to do it. It's not the first time they've spoken to me. They told me to do things. Most of the time, they offer random, inconsequential advice, where to go or what to have on the menu, but they usually speak to me at a point of indecision, which I must admit has been somewhat helpful. I welcome the small interruptions of insanity. But that's not to say I've forgotten who I am.

I'm not sure how much of my personal distresses I've mentioned before, it's nothing I'm too proud of. I understand that my anger issues will never be fully resolved; it's just who I am; nothing satisfies. I can find no peace in anything. Admittedly I am a hardened cynic with no confidence in anyone; I just eek through each day with intermittent tantrums every so often. Usually, a loud scream in a baron area does the trick, although lately, I'm not afforded such a luxury. The hardest thing for me is keeping my episodes from my daughter. I don't want her to see me like this.

As you know, my mother has been living with me for some time now since my father's passing. The loss was tragic enough, and to endure mom's slow decline into senility has become too much to bear. I'm allowed no concentration!

I can't think!

My life, as I know it, is over. I don't deserve this, do I?

Many times I would stand beside her while she sat in dad's old chair, rotting. ROTTING in that chair! I guess the feel of something of his was a comfort to her. She never moved, never made a sound, just would stare at the TV all day. I scarcely think she was even watching it half the time; everything around her ceased to exist. Even the joys of her granddaughter, my daughter, her little Hanna wouldn't merit a reaction. I finally confronted her, but my pleas were unheard. She would just stare right through me as if I wasn't even there. I've reached the end of my rope.

Yesterday, I had attempted to fix the back screen door, something I had put off for some time. The volume on the TV was so loud I felt the speakers might blow out. Clearly, she had moved. She had the remote, she turned it up, and in my head, I only thought this was done to intentionally irritate me. With my tools in hand, I approached my mother and asked her if she was okay again and again—still nothing. I finally felt my madness welling.

I let go of my tool bag and let the metal's weight fall hard onto the ground. It caused a clatter that was ear—shattering. It hurt me, but I didn't want to miss any flinch she might've given. I stifled the pain, gritting my teeth, remembering then Hanna was still upstairs. Her door was closed, but she heard it.

The next thing I remember is hearing them say to me, "Go back," and I was standing over my mother holding the hammer in such a way it felt more like a weapon than a tool. A wave of calm came over me until I realized what I had done. The claw end of the hammer was imbedded in my mother's head. In my mind, I had not done this, but all accounts will say I did. Whatever illusions, or feelings I had, had disappeared. My shock gave way to worry, thinking now of Hanna, and how I couldn't allow her to see this. I wish they would speak to me now; I could use the advice.

I had gotten to her door upstairs just as she was coming out. I don't know if she had noticed my hysterics at the time, but I quickly moved her back in to her room. I could see she was upset, but my efforts to calm her only seemed to confuse her further, and she began to cry. She grew more and more upset, flailing around wildly until I could no longer hold her still. All I could do was hug her. I did so tightly until she finally was quiet and still. She will understand what happened, one day. One day I'll tell her what had happened and why it was the decent thing to do.

She's been sleeping since yesterday. Even now, sitting next to her now, writing this, I'm finding it difficult to cope. I managed to stand a moment ago, the first time in hours, and I noticed that the house is as quiet as it's ever been. Even my head, quiet—they're gone, and I once again find myself at a crossroads. So often they have come to help me; however, I feel they've abandoned me. Before I came back to finish this letter, I stood in the middle of the room crying. I felt lost; I guess I still do.

I think soon I'll take Hanna downstairs and the three of us will have one last meal together before I bring mom to her house. As far as I know, it hasn't been sold yet. It was my parents' home for almost fifty years; I know she'll like it there. I figure after, I'll pack up Hanna and head out.

By the time you get this, I'll already be on my way. I just need a friend—someone to talk to me, you know. I would really love to meet you face to face, and you can even meet my daughter! I've told her all about you. I hope it's not too much to ask. Until then, best wishes!

Your friend,

Brian Edward Cole

***

It had been a year since Amy began her correspondence with Brian. This was the twelfth letter in the exchange, and it read like none other she had received before. It was rather disturbing, and Amy didn't know exactly how to deal with such an unexpected and graphic confession.

Soon after the initial shock had finally subsided, it suddenly became apparent that she might be in considerable danger herself. Immediately, a surge of terror welled up within her. Amy found herself trying to recall the conditions of all her windows and doors of the house. It was a pleasant fall evening, and even with the two windows open upstairs a vicious chill ran through her body. With the sliding back door to the deck open, and the front door open as well, she felt increasingly vulnerable. *Could he really be on his way here?!*

Amy was certain that Brian would not be at his home, and with no picture to identify him all there was, was an address and her concerns. She found it hard to convince herself that the police would take the matter seriously. But still, she set her phone on top of the letter, thinking that might be a course of action to consider later. Right now, she felt it more pertinent to recheck all the doors and windows. Amy hurried upstairs and closed the window in the bathroom and the one in her daughter's bedroom, locking them. It was impractical to think of someone crawling through the upstairs windows, but she could relax her nerves a bit with any form of security. While she drew the blinds in her daughter's room, she left the bathroom's cracked a bit, just enough to get a clear view of the front yard and the driveway. Nothing was out of the ordinary from what she could see; only the occasional car passing by. Amy moved downstairs.

It was disappointing to her, feeling that she had to box herself in like this. The act of fortifying the house made her feel, in a sense, insecure and afraid. Being the only one in the house now, with her daughter Sadie out enjoying the day, it was understandable, but to Amy, it was a shot to her confidence. They were here to be happy, not to isolate themselves from society. Taking one more look around outside, front and back, Amy felt comfortable enough to breathe a sigh of relief.

Daylight was fading fast as Amy returned to the kitchen and picked up her phone to text her daughter. She knew Sadie was out with friends, probably for the night, but she only wanted to know she was okay:

"HEY HONEY, HOW'S THINGS GOING? YOU NEED ANYTHING?"

Something simple; the question was genuine; however, Amy was baiting her for a response. She couldn't remember whether or not she'd ever mentioned Sadie to Brian; it would be understandable, but did it matter, she wondered. He couldn't know about Sadie, but the thought of his actions, at least what his letter had suggested, echoed in Amy's mind when thinking about her own daughter. *This is silly*, Amy finally accepted, feeling she was over-indulging in the whole matter. With her phone in hand, she once again laid eyes on the letter, and again the thought of calling the police crossed her mind. Soon after, she put the matter to rest, tucking the pages into the corner drawer, filing them with the other letters she'd received from Brian; a pile of friendly communiques now looked like a stack of evidence. Finally, she convinced herself she might be overreacting and shut the drawer and put the matter out of mind.

After all this, she felt she could use a drink and retrieved a beer from the refrigerator. As the door swung shut, so too, a car door closing could be heard outside. At this point, she was familiar with the resonance of the area and could tell if someone was in her driveway or a neighbor, or just on the street. A quick glance through the blinds confirmed it, though. Someone was here. The motion sensor light over the garage had been tripped.

An odd late-model marron Oldsmobile had pulled in, and parked closely behind her car. A tall thin man, young-looking, perhaps in his early-thirties, with short black hair and a trimmed beard emerged from the driver's side, he too was unfamiliar. The man did a quick survey of the surrounding area before opening the back door. He appeared to be struggling with something, trying to heft it out from the back seat. It was then that the same wave of terror took control of her body. The possibility had suddenly become more probable, yet she still found it hard to accept the notion of such an extreme situation. At odds with herself,

Amy didn't know whether to confront her visitor or call the police. Standing close to the counter, she watched, her muscles ridged, frozen in place, perhaps mercifully so, unable to draw any attention to herself.

The man pulled out a large object wrapped in a white floral blanket. At first glance, it looked like a child's blanket one might find in a crib. He seemed to be struggling a bit, shifting the weight of it from one arm to that other. It seemed heavy as the man had to reset the weight in his arms several times. Eventually, he cradled it like holding a sleeping child. Amy couldn't see what it was, but a cold chill rippled through her body, and her breath froze in her chest; the assumption was prevalent.

While the light of the kitchen no doubt gave her away through the open blinds, she remained still and watching as the man walked behind the wall, out of view before his steps could be heard thumping on the porch. They ceased, and Amy stood in paralyzed silence. For a moment, she could sense him leering through the wall before hearing the man wrap gently on the storm door...

KNOCK-KNOCK!

GOING MY WAY

A walk this long made an otherwise peaceful wilderness into a looming tranquil threat. It was serene, deceptively so, considering the circumstances, until the last remaining hues of blue was drained from the sky. The temperature was dropping quite fast for this time of year, and although September nights were almost always cool in upstate New York, Jonus Knolls was surprised to see his breath. After walking several miles for the last two hours, give or take, a frosty pinch began to sting his nose and ears. His strides became ridged and heavy, with his hands firmly in his jacket pockets and his chin tucked close to his chest. Though there was almost no wind, the cold crippled his joints and made looking up a painful task.

Not a soul in sight, civilization was a distance away in all directions. For the last two miles, or at least what felt like two miles, hell, it may have been three or four; Jonus hadn't heard or seen a trace of anyone in the area. No lights in the horizon or peering through the thick, surrounding forest, nor could he remember seeing any road signs; it was as if this road was cut through the woodland for no reason. There wasn't a town or city nearby, nor was there any indication of such. Not so much as a speed limit sign. It was dark, and if not for the moon being as bright as it was, he very well may not have made this attempt to find help.

A sudden breeze kicked up and tore through the leaves. But when nature fell silent, something else rose in the distance. Jonus stopped dead in his tracks to listen intently; to be sure the wind and the exhaustion weren't playing tricks on him. It fooled him earlier, but no, this was something different, definitely mechanical. As the noise grew closer and more defined, Jonus spun around with a glimmer of hope; his legs desperate for a reprieve.

On the other side of the hill, a soft glow dispersed in the fog and grew brighter as a vehicle crested. Jonus waited with eager alertness, as the headlights came into view. The sudden flare of light blinded him for the moment, obscuring his vision of anything except two white orbs heading his way.

Jonus took a conscious step into the road, waving his hands attentively and invasively, ignoring the pain that pulsed in his hands and limbs.

As it approached, the car decelerated and came to a stop while Jonus was in mid-stride, walking briskly toward the passenger's side. He approached and knocked on the window, waving at the dark figure in the driver's seat. He tried the door, but it was locked. The windows didn't seem to be tinted, but no light reached the interior. The driver sat in an ominous silhouette. Before Jonus could address the driver, the lock unlatched; Jonus hesitated a moment before climbing in.

"Thanks," Jonus said. His body immediately fell heavy, and relaxed in the chair. "Oh man, feels like I've been walking forever." Jonus shut the door, and they pulled away.

Even now, sitting next to him, it was difficult for Jonus to see his face. Despite being cloaked in the shadows, he could see that the driver was wearing a dark, long-sleeved jacket made of an unusual soft fabric, not denim or leather or any ridged cloth; it draped over his arm much like a thin bathrobe would. His hand's skin was quite pale, almost a chalky completion, but that's all Jonus could make out without making an obvious intrusive effort. To lean over and examine his face would be a bit out of place, he figured.

"Where are you heading?" the driver asked in a dark, brooding tone. His voice was raspy, sounding like that of a smoker in his late seventies accustomed to a two-pack a day habit.

After a brief pause, Jonus responded, "If I can get to a gas station, I can get a tow truck to take me back."

"Back where?"

Jonus was a bit confused as to the reason for such a question and, judging from the driver's tone, he opted not to answer. For several dragged out minutes, which seemed to expand with every passing mile, they sat in silence; the endless stretch of blacktop cutting through the wilderness looked to go on forever toward nothing. Even a kind passerby's assistance, there was no end to the road, which made Jonus all the more restless.

Finally, Jonus reached over and offered his hand: "Name's Jonus."

The driver was unwelcoming, not so much as turning a curious glance at his passenger, leaving Jonus's hand hanging there for a few seconds until he awkwardly pulled it back. As he settled back into his seat, Jonus casually turned his eye toward the driver, less concerned about his etiquette. But still, he could only make out the paleness of his skin, which was pronounced brightly by the moonlight.

Jonus patted down his pockets, trying to occupy himself out of this uneasiness. *Shit, I must've left my cigarettes back in my car*, Jonus thought. He turned to the driver, but before he could ask, the driver was already holding out an open pack of smokes with one ejected for Jonus to take. A curious expression came across Jonus's face. *How could he know what I was looking for?* He dismissed his apprehension and accepted the cigarette. With it hanging from his lips, Jonus searched his pockets again. As before, the driver presented him with a lighter, striking the flint to get Jonus's attention. Jonus hesitated for a second, before leaning forward to singe the end of the cigarette.

"Thanks," Jonus said with the cigarette hanging from his mouth. Opening the window a crack, Jonus relaxed into the seat, and took a few laid back, lung-filling breaths of smoke while still trying to assess his whereabouts. He watched out the window, the smoke from his breath and cigarette being torn from the car through the small opening in the window, as the endless scroll of trees rushed by in a blurring ribbon.

After yet another muted stretch, Jonus again tried to break the ice, "So," he started, with a nonchalant tone, "what brings you out this way? You're the first car I'd seen in, like, two hours."

The driver still didn't respond, staring intently out the windshield as if not having heard him. Jonus, now feeling a bit of uneasiness in his stomach, leaned away from the driver, retreating into his own bubble and resting his weight on the door. Looking down the distance of the road, which still showed no signs of life anywhere, Jonus grew more nervous as the minutes continued to pass, and the silence dragged out.

Jonus continued his attempts to steal subtle glances, but nothing distinguishable could be made out. The tension began to suffocate Jonus, as if the seatbelt were tightening around his chest, until the driver finally spoke,

"Tell me of your regrets," he said in the same haunting manner, as if reading from a prearranged and somewhat personal questionnaire.

Jonus was caught off guard, having exchanged almost no dialogue since being picked up. It was a little vexing to be asked something so personal.

"What do you mean?" Jonus asked as casual as he could sound.

"Do you feel bad about the things you've done?"

Jonus thought a moment, "What is it you think I did?" he retorted, confused.

The driver fell quiet again, perhaps waiting patiently for Jonus's answer. Not a sound, or look or a reaction, Jonus stared across the bench seat, trying harder now to get a look at any features of the driver's face. After taking a final drag of his cigarette, he snuffed it out in the ashtray.

"You know, I appreciate the ride," Jonus said with an air of arrogance, "but the random interrogation is making me a bit uncomfortable. So, why don't we keep the conversation to the general pleasantries, yeah?"

The driver gave a slow, gentle nod of acknowledgment. Jonus held his gaze of imposed authority before turning back to face the windshield. He remained in his own world while tending to his nails, picking out the dirt imbedded beneath them. His hands were rough and chapped, stained brown from mud that began flaking off. Jonus casually brushed himself off and cinched his coat a bit tighter to try and get warm.

"Cold night isn't it?" the driver commented.

"I guess that's life in the mountains," Jonus blandly replied.

"Do you think they'll ever be found?" the driver asked.

The question seemed out of place as Jonus tilted his chin toward the driver, leaning slightly away, doubt welling up in his eye. As bizarre as it was, it did have an impact; Jonus tensed up, his breathing became soft and drawn out.

"What are you talking about?" he asked, trying his best not to sound guilty.

"You don't forget. You're not allowed to forget," the driver said calmly, allowing Jonus to recall what had happened.

Jonus stared for several moments, searching his mind desperately for a denial. While immediately, he truly did not know what the driver was referring to, he knew his guilt; that sinking feeling inside him, as he tried to subdue any telling signs. "I didn't..." Jonus said softly, as images began to flash before his eyes—a man and a woman. Her face, though pretty fell to shock, looking back at Jonus. *The woman; who was she?* I can see her face. Even in his vision, she was looking at him. "I don't know them."

The driver slowly turned to Jonus, "Yes, you do," he assured in a whisper. He fixed his gaze on Jonus, never losing control of the car despite the abrupt tight curves. Images continued to enter Jonus's mind, painting a gruesome tale about a young couple who fell upon a grizzly misfortune. It came to him from his own point of view, watching himself interacting with an energetic young woman, so attractive that she could have her pick of the men in the room. She wasn't nervous at all about expressing her sexuality toward him. It was all so unreal. She was too beautiful to be talking to him. Jonus wondered if this was a subconscious fantasy, or reality.

Jonus' memory started coming back together, but he was unable to connect this occurrence to his current predicament. In fact, he had all but forgotten about why he was here in the first place. *Where was my car? What was I doing? Where was I heading?* These questions repeated over and over in his head, in an odd progression, the swirl of imagery continued to flood his mind.

The smell of her perfume, the beer, the smoke; it all became more prevalent in the car as if he were reliving the moment. It became more than just memories; it was tangible—real. The car grew quiet; all sound seemed to drain from it as the flirtatious young blonde continued to invade Jonus's mind. He had followed the voluptuous woman around the bar; their courtship growing rapidly, as they laughed and pawed at one and other until a mutual lust was attained.

The episode brought him to a dark moonlit room, staring up at the woman from the bar as she saddled over him. The throws of passion enveloped him, as he continued to be pulled through the memory. Just as quickly as the experience came into his mind, it was soon interrupted by another. He watched as a man entered the room and lunged for him, the woman leaping to the side to avoid the onslaught. Several punches were thrown between the two until Jonus found his advantage. In an outburst of rage, perhaps an effort to defend himself further, he continued to pummel his attacker until there was no more movement. The blood pumped heavily through his veins and pulsed in his hands, and the adrenaline surge kept his heart racing violently. The sensation was so great that Jonus slipped in and out of the dream-like state with each heartbeat, his breathing becoming increasingly erratic and short.

Jonus knelt over his motionless victim, staring down at his knuckles, which were now stained with blood. Below, the mangled face of his attacker was a crimson mask, unrecognizable. The woman cowered in the corner, under the bed cover, waiting for the chance to flee for her life. Jonus turned, and pursued her for a few strides before catching and bringing her to the ground. He felt the pressure in his hands, as if he were reliving the experience. He tried to silence her, his hands wrapped tightly around her neck, holding her firmly to the ground. She gagged for breath, clawing at his arms and face, actions that Jonus continued to feel. She continued to flail and jerk around, trying to get free until there was nothing more. All was still, quiet... time frozen in place.

Jonus woke from the dream; a frightened expression dressed his face, looking to the driver who remained calm, now with a fixed gaze out the windshield. He tried to close the window, but the mechanism was not functioning, and Jonus became cold again. Even more so this time, as if nothing were protecting him from the rush of the icy atmosphere. The crisp, cutting feel of the winter air blew right through him, as he once again began to see his breath.

The car fell dark, and Jonus found himself drawn into another paralyzing vision.

The smell of the fresh pine, the cold air... he was in the woods. The strain in his arms, he felt his body attempting to push two heavy bags into a crudely dug hole out in the middle of the forest. There wasn't enough light to see what they were, but after a few shoves, they rolled over and fell in. The bags tumbled and tore on a slide of exposed jagged rocks, and Jonus got a clear view of the bodies—one of the arms nearly falling out of a hole cut in the side of the bag. An overpowering sense of panic washed over him, as the hole was covered, one muddy shovel full at a time.

Only when the deed was done had he calmed. The nightmare was over, and Jonus found himself quietly inspecting his fingers again. There was indeed a thick grit of dirt wedged deep under his gnawed fingernails. The last disembodied image he saw was of himself driving, speeding down the road they currently occupied. But it was there the memory ended. Like reaching the last page of an engrossing book, Jonus wanted... *needed* to know more! What had happened in that missing gap of time? His breath trapped in his chest, not sure now who or what he was.

"Who the hell are you?" Jonus asked under his breath, attempting to hide his panic. The driver didn't respond, so Jonus asked again, this time more forceful, "HEY! Who are you?"

Jonus' fear and impatience got the better of him, after yet another question went ignored. He tried to open the door, not concerned with the car being in motion, but it was locked.

"I've had enough," Jonus stated, and then commanded, "I want out. Pull over!"

Still ignoring Jonus, the driver sped up. The engine roared as it worked to pull the car up the hill sent a surge of adrenaline through Jonus's system. This time Jonus tried the door again, with the committed intention of jumping out. The door was indeed locked, but now Jonus noticed there was no latch or button to be unlocked. His hands started to shake, as he pulled on the handle even harder, throwing his weight into the door. It didn't budge at all.

"It never ceases to amaze me," the driver said calmly, "how easily people can forget about the shadows they cast. And how surprised they are when they come back to haunt them."

Jonus tried the door several more times before the shimmering of flashing lights up ahead caught his attention. The driver slowed to a crawl as they approached.

Several police cruisers obscured the view, but once they were passed, the grim details became clear. The dark sedan had lost control over the tight curve and ran into the cliff's wall, which ran the length of the road for several miles. There was something familiar. White smoke trickled out from what was left of the front end; it looked like a crushed soda can. The fire crew had removed the driver's side door, which was now beside the car, on the ground. Several feet ahead of the wreck, paramedics were loading a gurney into the back of the coroner's van. Jonus felt like an anvil had suddenly dropped on his chest. He looked down and found his shirt stained a dark red, and a slight dab with his fingertips revealed his suspicion. He looked back on the scene. He had a clear view of a body bag resting on the gurney before the van doors shut.

As they passed by the roadblock, leaving the scene behind them, Jonus turned back to the front of the car, his mouth agape. His eyes staring down trapped in horrible thought. It took a moment for it to sink in before he could turn to face the driver.

"I'm here for your salvation," the driver said.

"This isn't right," Jonus argued silently to himself with impending dread in his tone. "I just—I, I just needed a ride," he said, lost in his own thoughts, trying to convince himself his thinking was wrong. He had to be wrong; he *needed* to be wrong.

It was then; the ground and the cliff-side began to crack all around them, as if the land itself was crumbling into a void. The asphalt started to fracture, and despite the road breaking apart, they never lost pace.

"Let me out!" Jonus screamed while attempting to shove the door open. "HEY!"

Suddenly, the surrounding sounds dissipated. There was no engine, no rush of the wind, or cracking of earth. Everything was silence. Jonus froze. The driver turned to him, now leaning into the light to where Jonus could finally see his face. His skin as pale as his hands; dried and cracked and formed to his skull, with his eyes sunken in and shriveled, an expired corpse, the wind tore apart his long white hair; the driver's voice became the only thing Jonus could now hear.

"You see," the driver stated, "nothing is ever forgotten. And on your judgment, the path which you lay in life, will be the one you walk..." he finished in a low, throaty tone, "...in death."

The driver smiled, revealing a row of rotten black teeth, as his eyes sunk into his skull. The hollow sockets a deep darkness, while what was left of his skin withered and flaked off like burnt tissue paper.

Jonus screamed as the skin flakes flooded the car. The wind rushed around to extreme velocities, throwing the car into a ravenous wind tunnel. Jonus watched the driver deteriorate next to him into a flawless skeleton. His clothes torn to shreds with the seat and entire driver's side covered in blood and flesh. He tried to distance himself as far as he could, pressed against the door, his body now configured to the car's shape.

A sudden, deafening implosion sent a shockwave from the ground. The concussion of which resonated through Jonus' body, forcing the air from his lungs. He looked ahead to see the road falling into an ever-expanding pit of fire and nothingness.

Bearing down further into the darkness, swallowed by the earth, the fire began to engulf the car. The heat increased all around as the interior ignited, the glass and metal melting away almost instantly. Jonus' screams carried nowhere, as if he were drowning, while grotesque hands, dripping of white-hot molten liquid emerged from the surrounding flames.

The car was incinerated, and Jonus was alone, as the demonic hands reaching for him, grabbing at whatever limb they could. They grabbed hold of an arm, melted it away from his body, and pulled it into the fire. Jonus' tortured cries became more confined, as the roaring blaze closed in with the hands reaching and clawing for more; a leg, then his jaw. The pain never lessened, nor did he fall into a merciful shock. Only constant agony, as the hands peeled away what was left of Jonus, until his screams dissolved to nothing.

***

Once the paramedics finished loading the gurney into the van, they slammed the barn doors shut and climbed into the cab. Up ahead, a police officer stood out of the way to stop any oncoming traffic, letting the paramedics drive on past the barricade.

A few hundred yards ahead, the road was unblemished, pristine. The van ran over what sounded like a forged piece of metal as they continued on into the night.

The flat, rectangular piece of scrap metal; it was the only thing left on this perceived plane, danced off to the side of the road and settled in the dirt. The license plate was unrecognizable, charred to blackness lost in the brush.

For a sneak peek into the continuation, and finale of Sacrifices Incarnate, here is the first chapter from:

Confinement

There are things that shame a town in such a way where all people come to agree, albeit in a hushed manner (not without irony), on a code of silence. This was the case with 23 Northfolk Drive in Poughkeepsie New York, which became the worst case of family tragedy since the Defeo murders of Amityville in 1974. Many of the residents of the town today react to the stories passed down, aided by the sight of the dilapidated structure. It has become a piece of land forgotten—"ignored" would be a better word. Not even daring, mischievous kids would approach it.

Despite its damning presence on the block, the neighborhood was quaint and pleasant. Folks in town were not used to any disruptions, much less a rouge car speeding down the quiet road. Thankfully, the children, most of them, were in school. The rest were off the street, out of harm's way as the car peeled around the soft bend in the road. If there was anyone unaware of its presence, they knew now. The car slowed and came to a sudden stop, only a few doors away from the haunting edifice. The driver seemed to pause in the middle of the road, long enough for any curious eyes to peel back their respective shades to get a look.

A young woman of her early thirties sat behind the wheel of the car, staring blankly at the house, until her courage was enough to move closer. She moved up the block at a crawl, closing the distance an inch at a time until she was parked in line with the front door.

She sat quiet, looking through the window, the still remaining divide between her and the domineering abode. From here, the overhang of the porch shaded the area as such, making it appear like a mouth waiting to engulf her. In a manner, she felt like it would again. This was her house; it was where she had killed her family.

The young woman, Tina Modell, was hesitant at first, but managed to exit the car, leaving it running in the middle of the street. It didn't matter, it wasn't hers. Tina stood up, keeping the car between her and her house, with a fixed fearful eye on the door. Staring into its looming blackness, the house seemed to grow in size, as if it were trying to engulf her. Standing in its shadow, she thought she could hear the structure groan and creak, seemingly reaching for her. Tina wanted to move closer, but had to break eye-contact.

Looking up and down the street, she didn't see any other cars, or any of the prying eyes, leering through camouflaged blinds. It had been some time since anyone had laid eyes on the haunt for more than a few accidental seconds. This time people watched with intention and curiosity, afraid to do so, as well.

Tina was unconcerned with the other people, now on the slow cautious approach to the front door. She moved into its deepened shade from the sun, feeling the temperature drop significantly with each step. It felt like a wintery terrarium under the houses' shadow, in an otherwise warm summer day. As Tina drew closer, the house itself groaned; perhaps the structure further succumbing to its age and condition, but it sounded like something more. Almost alive. Still, she pressed on.

Coming up to the porch, Tina felt she was stepping into the past, into its cold, grim grip. It was a memory she had to live with, but not one she cared to relive. Not bothering to look over the porch, her focus was set, as she approached the door. The instinct to knock fluttered in her mind, going so far as to raise her hand slightly.

Come in, child...

Tina paused; the feeling was overwhelming, slightly undercut by the doors sudden shutter of life. Having broken free from its rusted slumber, the door creaked open a few inches, like a heavy castle door being let open for the expected Constable. Tina pushed it the rest of the way, and entered.

It was dark, much darker than she had expected. The interior had long since been ransacked; what wasn't stolen was turned over and destroyed. There wasn't one area of the house that wasn't seized by a no doubt angry mob, fueled by their outrage at her crime. What would they think of her reemergence now? It didn't matter; Tina knew she didn't have long. It was only a matter of time. She continued through the house.

It was a surreal sight, her eyes' running over a life that once was, and yet there was no remorse for what she had done. Tina walked through seemingly without a care, but on a mission. She was looking for something. Moving through what was once the dining room, Tina stepped over the remnant of furniture, a table that held no apparent memory of any happy time. No flutter of holiday dinners, or special occasions took her away from the horror in the moment. You can see it, can't you?

The images of her mother and father faded in and out of her mind, feeling as though she was watching a nondescript recap of her life, but she was nowhere to be seen. Was it a memory? Tina didn't know. It was so unspecific in detail. Her mother, walking to and from the kitchen with no words or actions to go on, but it almost looked as though she had noticed Tina. However, Tina rationalized; it could have just been her imagination. She ignored the images, and moved on, and as soon as she had, they faded away.

Tina continued through the house, coming now to the staircase leading upstairs. She didn't hesitate, taking each step tentatively slow, now getting a better feel for her being here. What started as a guiding intuition was now becoming more of a focused intent. Though she always knew what she was after, she had no idea why, until now.

"I knew it, then," Tina said quietly. "You were there. When it happened, you were there."

…

Tina came to the landing and rounded the sharp corner to her old room. It, too, had been vandalized by people; the first thing Tina had noticed was her door, it had been kicked off the hinges. It lay on the floor at an odd angle, like a floating bridge into the room. Tina entered, carefully, looking down as not to trip over it, or any of the crumbled drywall that had been torn from the wall. Looking around at the destruction, she was more confused at her lack of emotion towards her childhood room, rather than what had happened. She began to put the pieces together.

Standing in the middle of the room, she felt as though she were looking on these walls for the first time with new eyes. "You're here, now. Aren't you?" Tina said, near rhetorical. She was convinced, not fully, but almost. She continued to look around, like her visual range was always just short of whomever she was talking to. "I know you're here."

Indeed, I am, child.

"You were here, that night, too," Tina said matter-of-factly.

Looking around the room, Tina's eyes found a rusted vent in the corner of the room where her bed used to be. It was what she had come searching for. Tina moved to the corner and crouched down, and immediately went to work on the grate. It didn't take much prying, and Tina was able to pull it free. She pondered, as her hands touched something in the vent—that her secret had survived. But, she felt confident enough, reaching her hand into the vent. She felt around a minute, before retrieving a yellowed envelope, and a sleeve of dust and spider webs. Thankfully, for her sake, there was nothing she could see crawling within.

Tina examined the envelope a moment, amazed that it was still intact after all these years. It was the first time she had felt any emotion since arriving at the house, so much so, as a small welling of tears gathered in her eyes. She didn't have long to ponder, though. Outside, a slight commotion drew her attention away. Tina rose to her feet to look out the window.

There, she saw two sheriff's cars, and an ambulance pull up out front. They immediately exited, and approached the house, falling quickly out of view as they came up onto the porch. She could soon hear their footsteps entering the house, and one of the men calling out, "Sheriff's department!" Tina wasn't scared, but rather annoyed at their presence, having wished she had a little more time. "Ms. Modell, if you're here, please announce yourself. This doesn't have to be any more unpleasant than it already is, okay?" He sounded accommodating enough, and Tina headed out of her room.

The two sheriffs came to attention, hearing the floorboards creaking upstairs. They held their guns at the ready, but not as to intimidate anyone. They were more cautious than threatening. Looking up the stairs now, Tina came into view, as calm as they could have hoped. "Alright, Ms. Modell, I want you to show me your hands, and come down the steps slowly, okay?" he spoke as though he were talking to a nine-year-old who was lost and afraid. They just wanted to take her home. In a sense, that was the case.

Tina had spent the years in an asylum for her heinous crime, kept in a near-catatonic state, until just recently. The last few nights have been plagued by an incessant urge to return home, but she knew of no apparent. However, clutching the weathered envelope in her hand, she had found what she was looking for.

As she approached the sheriff, she became increasingly agitated; one hand on the gun, the other reaching for her arm. "That's right, Tina," he said calmly, though the anxiety was clear in his voice. The other sheriff waited close by, alert, and ready to act. Only inches away, the sheriff closed the distance quickly, and grabbed at her arm with a vice-like grip. His touch triggered an expected, but hazardous reaction.

Tina instantly flipped attitudes, thrashing and screaming incoherently. Both men closed in, attempting to subdue her. It took all their effort to ground Tina and close her hands behind her back, and her ankles together. "It's okay. You're okay," they reassured her. "We're just going to get you outside, okay, and get you back to the hospital." Their voices were calming, strangely contrast to the manic actions taking place.

"NO! NO!" Tina screamed, "He's here! He will find me! Please!"

Her calls fell on deaf ears, as the sheriffs were finally able to bind her wrists and ankles with zip ties. They held their knees on her shoulders and legs for a few moments waiting on the paramedics.

Once they gave the all-clear sign, two paramedics entered and quickly sedated Tina. Though she didn't fall asleep, she was near unresponsive, and would be so for the rest of the day. She was then loaded onto a gurney and wheeled out of the house.

The sheriffs stood up to catch their breath, looking down at what was in Tina's hands. The envelope lay at their feet. "This is what she came here for?" one of them commented.

"Who knows with that one, really?"

They both hissed out a relieved sigh and exited. Not knowing anything of horror left behind.

You know nothing of what is... You can never know.

The story behind the stories

No Fracking

This story was probably the easiest one for me to visualize, as it was based on the Catskill Motel, in Liberty New York. On a trip upstate to visit Howes Cavern, among other prominent sight-seeing locations, I found myself in a rather rundown location.

I remember getting a look at the area, and thinking that this isn't the kind of place you want to be stranded in. That's how the story started. The dilapidation of the room, and the exterior stuck with me, and is written accurate to the time. Though, I've seen recent pictures, and it looks like it's been renovated to a great degree. Perhaps this book will make its way up there, and bring with it a story to tell.

The obvious fiction of the story is the tar monster; however, the inspiration for the title is steeped in fact, as the area was riddled with ambiguous warnings of "No Fracking". One such warning was indeed painted on a decrepit truck on the side of the road. I guess these images stuck with me all these years.

"untitled"

The fifties creature horror spectacle was something of a groundbreaking time. Oh, how I wish I could have been around then to witness the moment to moment impact it had on audiences around the world. I know at the time they were kind of scowled at, and underappreciated. Nowadays, we look on these films as classics; milestones of the genre.

I guess it was my desire to make something as ambiguous and unknown as those films. I wanted to leave as much as I could unanswered, allowing you to debate among yourselves what this creature could be. Where did it come from? Not even I know that! My only concern was coming too close to The Blob. Looking back, I can see the subconscious influence, but I hope I kept enough of a distance. What did you think? Feel free to reach out and tell me!

Restless

Who doesn't have a fear of being buried alive? Simple enough, I think most can agree. But I have always been fascinated by the old timey tales of graves being outfitted with bells in case of such a traumatic happening. God, what would someone in that predicament go through?

Well, if someone were so unfortunate, at least they would have death to look forward to as an eventual release, albeit a terrible one. Not this story, though. I don't grant such luxuries!

The Emptiness

This was one such story that went through a number of title changes. There was "The Quiet Ones", "The Darkness", "Silence". Needless to say, it was a bone with little meat on it.

However, the practice of meditation has been one something I started learning more about several years ago. It has been very rewarding, but at the same time, depending on your beliefs, I suppose, there is a degree of vulnerability that comes with it.

In this story, I provide such an ominous presence that could disrupt those peaceful moments. I hope this doesn't put any of you off meditation. There's nothing to fear... is there?

The More You Gnome

Be honest, how many of us have passed by the garden section in the local hardware store and not given those creepy little things a second glance? You know you do, if only for a second! Well, I figure, why not breathe some actual life into these unassuming creatures?

They look so innocent, so friendly; maybe our presumptions are influenced by the Keebler elves, or some other cartoon. Nice enough they are, sure, but what if they became hostile? Huh? Might make you think twice the next time you consider such arbitrary décor for your flower bed!

The J.A.R

My crack at the sci-fi realm; you might find get a bit of a "Black Mirror" vibe. At least, that's what has been brought to my attention thus far. For that, I am grateful, as it was a contributing influence. But, one of the things that scare me the most is not having any control over anything when I'm dead. I know what you're thinking, "but you're dead. What does it matter?" That's kind of the point.

What if something could be done to "preserve" you? Would you do it? What's more, would you want someone/something you could not see, feel, or hear in control of your life? Well, who knows? Maybe we are living in such a Justifiable Artificial Reality right now.

Collateral

You have to love a good Mob story. The unseen hands that reign over all things we take for granted. Well, sort of. These stories always get my blood going, be it a tragic tale, or a coming of age one. But they always want one of two things: money, or power! And they usually get it, for a time.

In a way, I wanted to make a different kind of story. Noe that asks, if you had nothing to external to offer for a loan, would you put up a body part? If so, which one, and what's it worth to you? I know guys are cringing; sorry, it had to be done!

A Murder

What started out as a contest short story evolved into a better one, perfect for this anthology. The rules of the contest were what helped me direct it in a different narrative. No dialogue was allowed, but without such a restriction, it was determined that a few lines here and there would help convey the emotions better.

When panic strikes, we are all capable of things we would normally never do. And those things usually take us down roads we never knew existed. Roads that we would just as soon like to forget.

Pen Pal

How well do you really know someone? What does it mean to get to know someone? Sure, everyone has their secrets, and we are all comfortable enough to leave those dogs sleep soundly. But, what if you learned something about someone you couldn't unlearn? How would it affect your relationship?

I don't know if the "pen pal" is still a thing these days. But, I had one when I was younger, and it was quiet interesting from what I remember. However, there was always that reassuring veil of anonymity; a strange kind of trust can be developed. What if, however, that faceless, anonymous stranger told you a secret like this, and was coming to see you?

Going My Way

I don't know why the phrase "going my way" stuck with me. The tired, somewhat campy inquiry in requesting a ride has a certain ring to it, doesn't it? Or is that just me?

Hitchhikers themselves, have always come with their own level of skepticism, as do the generous drivers. Contrary to the "Pen Pal", there is no inherent trust, but rather weary suspicion on both parts. Well, that's what we have here. I have never hitched a ride, and probably never will. I once asked a ride of the plow truck drivers in a snow storm to retrieve my car. If that counts, I stand corrected. How about you? Have you hoped into someone's car for a ride across town, or the country? Tell us about it, and with all my gratitude, thank you for the read.

We hope you enjoyed the book.
Keep up with our latest projects and content at
The Horror Seeker.com/WordPress

Also, be ready for what's coming next:

KYN
Spring, 2021
and
Confinement – The second part to *Sacrifices Incarnate*
Fall, 2021

Made in the USA
Middletown, DE
07 September 2020

17352370R00116